LUKE STEVENS AND THE BLOOD OF ST GEORGE

BEN PEYTON

For my mum & dad
Dad, you are so missed

PROLOGUE

erlin, Germany 1940.

B The man's head throbbed from where they'd hit him. He'd regained consciousness about five minutes ago and was taking in his surroundings. As his swollen eyes adjusted to the dull light coming from the single bulb above him, his other senses began to catch up. He was tied to a wooden chair with his hands bound behind him and his feet roped together. His clothes were soiled with dirt and blood. Most of it his.

The ceiling and walls were made of stone and were slick with condensation. He couldn't see a door, so assumed it was behind him. The room was damp and he could taste the metallic tang of blood in his mouth. The latter was also encrusted to his face, around his nose and lips. The only sounds he could hear were a low buzz coming from the bulb and the occasional scream from outside the room. He could sense other people with him, but did not know how many. He had a feeling he knew where he was and hoped he was wrong.

How did he get here?

Of course. It was the woman.

A pushover for a damsel in distress, he knew it had to be because of her. He'd been driving in the rain when he'd noticed her struggling to change a tyre on her car by the side of the road. Without hesitation, he'd pulled over to help and had immediately been transfixed by her red hair and green eyes. So much so that he failed to hear the group of soldiers that had been lying in wait for him until it was too late. Although he gave almost as good as he got, he'd eventually been overpowered and bundled into a waiting car. They must have sedated him as he felt lightheaded and lethargic, or it could just be from the blow to the head he'd received. Either way, he felt groggy and disorientated.

With a wry smile, he wondered what the woman was doing now and whether she was thinking about him. Probably not, he concluded.

He was brought back to reality by the scraping sound of a bolt being drawn and a door opening. Footsteps echoed on the stone floor as someone approached him from behind. The flick of a switchblade caused him to flinch, but it was just to cut the ropes around his hands. He rubbed them together, attempting to ease the uncomfortable feeling in them.

A soldier in a high-ranking military uniform stood in front of the chair and regarded his prisoner.

"I shall speak to you in English, as we don't have much time. Or, rather, you don't have much time because soon you shall be dead," the officer said. "Do you know who I am?"

The prisoner appraised him for a few moments. He was of average height, had a slight paunch to his otherwise slim body, a weak chin, a thin moustache not quite extending to the edges of his lips and wore gold-rimmed glasses with large lenses.

"Yes, I think I do. You're the American president. It's an honour to meet you, President Roosevelt. I'd stand to greet you but I'm a little tied up."

The officer clenched his jaw.

"English humour, I presume. But you do not make me laugh. I know you know who I am."

"Then why the hell did you bother asking me, you fool?" the prisoner laughed and spat a wad of blood towards the officer which splattered one of his lenses. He calmly removed his glasses, produced a handkerchief from his pocket and wiped the blood away whilst, from behind the prisoner, a guard tilted back his chair and another rained punches onto his face.

As he replaced his glasses, the officer said, "Please do not do that again, Mr Stevens."

At the mention of his name, the prisoner looked slightly perturbed, but tried to hide it. The officer noticed and smiled.

"Yes, John. We know who you are and what you protect. You will tell me where it is."

"Go to hell."

"You are already in hell, John, as you will soon find out."

The two men stared at each other as the sound of the door opening again broke the silence. The officer immediately stood to attention and strode purposefully away.

A muffled conversation was taking place behind John, and he turned his head to see what was happening. His view was restricted, however, and all he could see was the back of the officer he had just been speaking with.

Looking forward once again, John sensed the atmosphere in the room change as a figure slowly made its way towards him. He suddenly felt very cold, and the hairs on his arms and neck began to rise.

A feeling of despair arose from deep within him and for the first time since he'd been brought to this place, John felt an emotion that he hadn't felt in a long time: fear.

His heart beat faster as the figure took his place before him. John was looking at the new arrival's feet and saw boots that were immaculately polished and blacker than the darkest night. The presence said nothing, letting the silence linger until John could stand it no more. He raised his head and his suspicions were confirmed.

He was indeed in hell.

And the Satan before him was Adolf Hitler.

PRESENT DAY

Luke Stevens grunted at his alarm clock to switch it off. The smart speaker continued its incessant buzzing and refused to listen to him. Admitting defeat, he rose from his bed and turned the stupid thing off manually, glaring at the 7:30 am display. So much for voice recognition.

He could hear his Aunt, Sarah, downstairs whistling to a song on the radio whilst she prepared breakfast. The aroma of toast and coffee did little to raise his spirits. The thought of going to school lowered them even more. Although Luke wasn't particularly academically gifted, his grades were above average and he worked hard to keep them that way. In a couple of years, he would have to make decisions about what he wanted to study after he left school. Luke had an interest in art and history so perhaps there was some mileage in exploring those options. Too bad there wasn't a course in PlayStation gaming for him to enrol in.

Luke had a quick shower and threw on his school uniform, doing his best to look as cool as a 13-year-old boy in a school uniform could. Unfortunately, the clothes weren't in the best condition. There were several patches where tears had been repaired and its once jet-black colour was now more of a shabby grey. His wavy, light brown hair was parted on the side and he had a fringe that kept falling over one of his startling blue eyes. Grabbing his bag, he went downstairs and was greeted by Aunt Sarah doing a crossword, munching on toast and slurping her coffee.

"The demon rises from his pit. Good morning, Prince of Darkness. Did you remember to close your coffin?" quipped Aunt Sarah, looking up from her paper.

"No, I thought I'd leave it open for you. After all, you're doing a crossword and listening to Magic FM. If you tell me you're going to Bingo tonight, I'll say my farewell now," retorted Luke.

"Touché. Help yourself to breakfast."

Luke poured himself a glass of orange juice and began buttering some toast.

"So, what's on for today? Double Latin followed by embroidery and cross-stitching or don't they teach those anymore?" joked Aunt Sarah.

"We're visiting the National Gallery as part of our history project."

"That's today?" Aunt Sarah looked up from her paper.

"Yes. I told you about it ages ago. You even signed my permission slip."

"Did I? Oh."

Luke smiled to himself at his aunt's memory lapse. Although she was in her early forties, she appeared much older. Not just in her looks, which were old-fashioned, and – he'd never say this to her face – frumpy, but in her person-ality and behaviour. She always wore her hair in a bun, usually sported an apron around her waist, even when she wasn't cooking, and had the habit of regularly pushing her black plastic-framed glasses further up her nose when they began to slide down.

Luke had come to live with Aunt Sarah five years ago, after his parents were killed in a car accident. Not a day went by where Luke didn't think about them several times. At first, he had found Aunt Sarah to be tedious and dull, but he soon warmed to her and now appreciated her for what she was, quirks and all.

Aunt Sarah had only met Luke a few times before he moved in, and even then, the meetings were brief. Single and not particularly comfortable around children, Sarah had struggled to engage with Luke until a mutual passion for art had brought the two closer together. Now, they were more like brother and sister than aunt and nephew.

"What are your plans for the day?" asked Luke.

"Well, the cushions need plumping, and I might look out of the window for a while. Oh, wait. I did that yesterday," she chuckled. "I've some business to attend to in town."

"What sort of business?"

"Just business, and I'll thank you to mind your own beeswax."

Luke laughed, finished his breakfast, and went to gather his school things. Just as he was about to leave the house, Aunt Sarah called to him.

"Enjoy the gallery. Why don't you check out Tintoretto's painting in room nine? It's one of my favourites. I'd be interested to hear your thoughts."

"Will do. I'll see you later."

"Oh, and Luke? Happy birthday." She threw him a present which he deftly caught.

"Thanks, Aunt Sarah, but you know how I feel about birthdays."

"Luke, I miss them, too. He was my brother. They'd want you to be happy."

"I am happy, Aunt Sarah. I just don't like birthdays."

There was a slightly uncomfortable silence between them.

"Fair enough. But I can still give you a present, right? Something tells me you'll like it."

Luke smiled. "Thanks. I'll open it on the bus. See you."

He turned and left the house, leaving Aunt Sarah smiling after him as she went back to her crossword.

Luke stared at the gift as he made the ten-minute bus journey to school. He put it in his bag, refusing to acknowledge that today was his birthday. It was five years ago to this day that Luke's parents were tragically killed. The present took him back to that dreadful morning when Aunt Sarah had turned up unexpectedly at his school and told him the awful news. Luke's parents were never coming home. Numb with grief and with only the distant Aunt Sarah to comfort him, Luke packed a few things from his house and, in a daze, went to live with her.

The two weeks leading up to his parent's funeral dragged on until, finally, they were laid to rest. Luke only knew Aunt Sarah at the service and was surprised to see at least twenty other people there. Luke, Aunt Sarah and his parents were the only members of his family that he knew of, so he assumed the others were his parent's work colleagues from their office where they used to be accountants. On that painfully dark day, Luke's thoughts also drifted to the two men he had seen standing far enough away from the service to not intrude, but close enough to pay their respects. One was small and old, but the other young, tall and powerfully built. Luke thought he recognised the older man as something about him seemed so familiar and he thought he saw Aunt Sarah smiling at the younger guy, but by the time several strangers had passed on their condolences to him, both had vanished.

The excited chatter of his schoolmates leaving the bus broke Luke's melancholy, and he joined the throng of children walking towards their school.

The journey into London and the National Gallery was uneventful. On the bus, Luke sat next to Charlie Hall. Charlie was slightly shorter than Luke, with curly brown hair, glasses that had a broken arm and an identical pattern of five freckles on each cheek, like a clown. He had a habit of biting his nails and an unhealthy obsession with *Star Wars*.

The two boys had befriended each other during an after-school chess club. Well, they didn't have a choice as they were the only two there. Like Luke, Charlie preferred his own company, but was more than happy to buddy up with Luke when the opportunity arose.

"I'm telling you that everyone wants to be Han Solo or Luke Skywalker, but they're not seeing the bigger picture. Darth Vader is the one to be. Think about it. He has the best costume, the best voice. Everyone remembers him and he kills the Emperor," enthused Charlie.

"True, but doesn't he also slaughter an entire group of children?" asked Luke.

Charlie looked at Luke, blinking in confusion. "Well,

um, yes, I suppose he does, but he redeems himself at the end."

"True again, but doesn't he also help blow up an entire planet which would've been full of more kids? Not to mention all those poor droids?"

Charlie's face paled and he floundered for a response. "You raise some valid points. Thank you for bringing them to my attention. I must rethink my ideas." He looked as though he might burst into tears.

Luke smiled, slapped him on the shoulder and said, "Come on, Anakin. Let's see what history's finest have for us." And with that, they followed their teachers into the building.

Mr Crocker, Luke's history teacher, was explaining to his students the day's itinerary in his usual nasal whine. Luke only heard snippets of it, as he was too busy taking in his surroundings. Feeling at home amongst so many pieces of art, Luke was eager to delve deeply into history's treasures and see what the National Gallery had to offer.

"Nice hair, Puke. Who cut it? Your mum? Oh, I forgot. She's dead, isn't she? Well, it must've been your aunt then. Your style's as old as she is."

Approaching Luke was Rick Tyler, surrounded by his usual entourage of smirking followers. Rick was ridiculously good-looking, captain of the school football team and, unfortunately, the headmaster's son. Rick had taken it upon himself to make Luke's life a misery when Luke had started at the school. He'd given up asking why.

Luke sighed and began to move away, but Rick grabbed his arm and spun him round so that they were facing each other.

"Don't walk away from me, freak." A ripple of appreciation moved through Rick's posse. Some boys in his group looked at Rick with awe whilst the two girls with him had hearts in their eyes.

Luke had learnt the hard way to ignore Rick's bullying. On the one occasion he had tried to stand up for himself, he'd ended up with a bloody nose and had his bus fare stolen. The walk home in the rain had given him a cold, and he'd missed two days of school. Aunt Sarah had wanted to speak to the headmaster but Luke convinced her it would probably do more harm than good.

The two boys stared at each other. "Do what you have to do and be on your way, Rick."

"Don't you ever tell me what to do, Puke," this earned another smattering of laughter. "You know, I've always wondered if your dad deliberately crashed his car because he was so ashamed of you, or maybe he just wanted to kill your mum because she'd got so fat and ugly."

At this, something deep inside Luke stirred. His fists clenched, and he ground his teeth so hard he thought they might break. Rick was high-fiving some of his friends when he heard a faint sound, almost animal-like, coming from Luke. He looked at his friends to see if they'd heard it, but they were too busy laughing at Rick's taunting.

The two boys made eye contact again. Luke's rage continued to bubble, and for the first time, he saw a flicker of doubt in Rick's eyes. His expression changed from fear to confusion and back to fear again. With false bravado, he announced they should, "leave the freak to his only friends; dead ones."

As the gang moved off laughing, Rick cast another look back at Luke. The reason for his fear? He could have sworn, just for a split second, that when he looked into Luke's eyes, he saw a flaming fire looking back at him.

Luke waited for Rick and his gang to disappear out of sight before releasing a long breath. His fists finally unclenched and he closed his eyes and concentrated on bringing his heart rate down to normal.

He'd heard the low, guttural growl that came from within him and had felt a euphoric sense of soaring confidence coming from every pore of his body as he'd squared up to Rick. As his breathing calmed, he began to feel confused and a little scared about what had just happened. He also felt light-headed and needed to rest his hands against a wall to right himself. He saw how Rick had looked at him and remembered his frightened face. Surely he hadn't imagined the whole thing? Rick had gotten bored with his game and decided to play elsewhere. That must be it. Still, as Luke walked back towards his teachers and the tour guide, he couldn't help but think of the sound he thought he'd heard. It was familiar, yet like nothing he could place.

Luke and his party walked up a set of marble steps to begin their tour.

"Founded in 1824, the National Gallery is home to some of Europe's finest works of art in a collection of well over 2,000 pieces. These range from the 13th century to the 20th century. You will see some of the world's most famous paintings by some of the world's most famous artists. Some you will already know, but others you will have the pleasure of seeing for the very first time. Oh, how I envy you! Now, before we enter the first room, are there any questions?" Their guide was a spritely, elderly Irishman called Patrick. He was short and had a spring in his step that contradicted his ageing appearance.

"Is it true that van Gogh only sold one painting in his lifetime?" asked a girl.

"Indeed it is, young lady. We'll see and hear more of Vincent as the tour continues."

"And did he really cut his ear off?" she continued.

"That he did. It was after an argument with his friend, the artist Paul Gauguin, over a woman. They'd been drinking a French alcoholic beverage called absinthe. When drunk in large quantities, which it was, absinthe has been known to produce hallucinations. Can't stand the stuff myself, I prefer a nice single malt whiskey. Bushmills if it's available, but I'm not particularly fussy. Where was I? Ah, yes. Vincent took a razor, sliced off his left ear, or part of it anyway, wrapped it in paper and took it to an establishment that he and Gauguin used to frequent when they were feeling particularly –"

A cough from Mr Crocker interrupted Patrick's story. "Perhaps we can learn more about van Gogh when we view his *Sunflowers* later in the tour?"

"Quite. Yes, of course. Well, the moral of the story is that absinthe doesn't make the heart grow fonder!" He giggled at his joke for several moments until he realised nobody else was laughing. "Absinthe makes the heart? Alas. Never mind. Well, moving on," continued Patrick, oblivious to any embarrassment he might have caused.

"Are there any paintings of dragons here?"

Patrick turned to see where the question had come from and saw Luke at the back of the group, with his hand in the air. The question had taken him by surprise and had left his mouth before he'd thought about it. Nobody paid him any attention apart from Rick, who was eyeing him suspiciously.

"As a matter of fact, we have three that spring to mind. Well, four, but one isn't currently on display. The four I refer to are of the same dragon. A rather famous dragon." Patrick didn't notice the disinterested looks from the children surrounding him and kept his focus solely on Luke. "Legend has it that a fierce and terrible dragon was terrorising a small village in Italy and to appease the beast, the villagers would offer it a regular human sacrifice." At this, some children began to show signs of life again.

"To prevent an uprising, the region's king decided to sacrifice one of his own family. His daughter, a princess. The princess was obviously not too pleased with this arrangement, but had no choice but to go along with it. She was taken to the dragon's lair and tied up to await her fate. Meanwhile, a Roman knight, believed to have been from Turkey, although we can't tell for sure, was passing through the area when he learned of the princess's plight. Appalled, he gallantly rode upon his noble steed towards the fair maiden, hoping to prevent the princess from becoming the dragon's next meal. He arrived just in the nick of time, fought magnificently, and landed a near-fatal blow on our fiery friend. The princess used her girdle as a leash and the subdued dragon was led back to the village where the soldier, a devout Christian, vowed to slay the beast if the villagers converted to his religion. They readily agreed and the entire community was baptised. The dragon was subsequently slaughtered by our hero and a church was built upon the site."

The children were looking at Patrick in a new light. He continued, "This is one of many interpretations of the famous legend and is, of course, complete balderdash, but a good yarn nonetheless. Now, we'll see more of that dragon as we continue our tour, so let's crack on."

"What was the name of the soldier who killed the dragon?" inquired Luke.

"Of course, how silly of me. Well, you all know him, without a doubt. The noble knight that slew the dragon and rescued the princess is none other than England's patron saint: George."

4

The rest of the tour passed by in a blur of watercolours and frames as Patrick did his best to pass on his wealth of knowledge to the group of disinterested youngsters. Thankfully, Rick kept his distance from Luke and, finally, Patrick led them to the last part of their visit.

"Here we are, as promised. *St George and the Dragon* by Jacopo Tintoretto. Believed to have been painted in about 1555, Tintoretto had a flair for the dramatic as you can clearly see. He spent most of his life in the beautiful surroundings of Venice. He loved living there so much, there's only one record of him ever leaving. Anyway, I'll leave you to enjoy the painting and I'd like to thank you for being such an attentive audience. I'll be hovering awhile here if you have any further questions." As he said this, his gaze lingered on Luke for a moment before he skipped away to look at the other paintings.

"Thank you, Patrick, for your enthusiasm and expertise," Mr Crocker shouted after the spritely man. "Okay, you lot. You have 15 minutes to look around this section and then we'll meet up right here and head back to the bus. Off you go!"

The group split up, heading in different directions, with Luke aiming for the Tintoretto. He was joined by Charlie.

"Well, Patrick was a character," he said. There was a brief pause as they took in the image of St George on his white horse thrusting a lance towards the dragon as a lady in a blue dress with a long pink shawl made her escape. "What do you think?" asked Charlie.

"I think there's more to Patrick than meets the eye."

"I meant about the painting."

"Oh. Well, he was right about it being dramatic. Look at that dead body lying there. And is that supposed to be God up in the sky? The castle's pretty impressive. What's with the writing on his lance?"

"There isn't any writing on his lance."

"Yes, there is. Look. It's like a faded silver, but I can't make out what it says. It could be Latin or something."

Charlie edged as close as he could to the painting and squinted. "Dude, are you crazy? There's absolutely nothing there."

"What? Yes, there is. Look closer."

"Any closer, and I'll have to take the lady in the blue dress on a date. Come on, let's head back."

As Charlie left to meet up with the rest of the school, Luke pulled out his phone and took a quick photograph of the painting. Staring at the image, he could clearly see, yet fail to read, what were very definite markings across St George's lance. Frowning, he pocketed the phone and made his way towards Charlie.

He failed to notice that Patrick had been standing near, listening to his exchange with Charlie, a look of assured amusement on his face.

On their way back to school, Charlie shared his ranking of the *Star Wars* films with a passion that was bordering on the insane. "A lot of people say that *The Phantom Menace* is the worst of them, but they're wrong. You've got pod races, Qui-Gon Jinn, a young Obi-Wan, a younger Darth Vader and Darth Maul. What's not to like?"

"Jar Jar Binks?"

"Why though? Granted, his voice is a little irritating, but he was for the kids as comic relief. It's only adults that don't seem to like him, but they didn't mind the ewoks in *Return of the Jedi* when they were kids, did they? Just as annoying, but they get a free pass. It makes no sense."

Luke zoned out as Charlie continued his ramblings, choosing to focus on the day's events. His encounter with Rick had unsettled him, probably not as much as it had Rick, but it was enough to concern him. That, along with the markings on St George's lance that Charlie couldn't see, had him thinking.

The bus arrived at their school and Charlie and Luke said their goodbyes, promising to do some online gaming at the weekend. Luke wasn't too far from home when someone came up from behind and shoved him to the ground. When he looked up, he saw Rick Tyler standing over him, fists clenched and furious.

"How dare you talk to me like you did in front of my friends! You embarrassed me. Nobody does that."

"What do you want now, Rick? Just leave me alone."

"No. I need to teach you a lesson and it starts now."

Luke stood up, leaving his bag on the ground.

"What have I ever done to you, Rick? Why me? Ever since we met, you've had it in for me when I've done nothing wrong."

"You exist. It annoys me. I don't like you. I never have, I never will."

"Right, well, that clears that up. Thanks for the in-depth explanation."

"You want a reason? Fine, I'll give you a reason. Two years ago in PE, we were playing football. You were in goal and my team had a last-minute penalty. I was on a hat-trick so I took it, but you saved it and we lost."

"This is all because I made you lose a friendly game of football? I don't even remember that! I hate football."

"See? That's why. It meant nothing to you, but it meant something to me. There were girls watching that game and you made me look stupid. Even though you won that, you're still a loser. Your aunt's a loser and your parents were the biggest losers of all."

There it was again. At the mention of his parents, that same feeling Luke had felt at the gallery began to simmer away inside of him. He ignored Rick's continued taunts and savoured the energy that seemed to consume him. It enveloped him, taking over his entire body. He closed his eyes, enjoying the warmth that was spreading through him. Nervous excitement seemed to find a home in every pore of Luke's body.

He opened his eyes to see Rick's fist hurtling towards his face. Time seemed to slow as Luke expertly avoided it, his surprise eclipsing even Rick's. Recovering quickly, Rick launched another punch towards Luke's stomach that, again, he promptly dodged, causing Rick to stumble forwards. Confused and enraged, Rick tried once again to attack Luke, this time running at him to take him down. As he drove his shoulder into Luke's chest, he was thrown to the ground by Luke in a move that knocked the wind out of him. Rick staggered to his feet, humiliation replacing anger as he caught his breath. Taking one last tired swipe at Luke, his fist was caught by Luke's hand, inches from his face. As the two stared at each other, Rick saw that Luke's eyes had once again changed and were glowing with a burning orange intensity. As Rick's fear grew, his arm was effortlessly lowered by Luke's vice-like grip. Tears filled Rick's eyes, and he began to whimper. Taking deep breaths, Luke began to return to normal, the feeling of power and confidence fading into the background.

"Leave me alone," he said to Rick.

Rick slowly nodded, muttered something that could have been an apology, and ran away faster than anyone has ever run before. Luke was left standing there, shocked yet overjoyed. What on earth had just happened to him? As Luke started to move off, he felt dizzy and tired. He quickly moved to a near-by bus stop and sat down before he fell down. Closing his eyes, he concentrated on breathing until the feeling passed. As Luke began to feel himself again, he started to chuckle, which quickly turned into a laugh. He gathered up his bag and found he was still laughing by the time he arrived home.

5

Opening the door and walking inside, he was greeted by Aunt Sarah, ending a telephone call. "Hello, you. How was The National Gallery?"

"Actually, it was really interesting. A real eye-opener," Luke said, unable to keep from smiling.

"That's wonderful to hear," replied Aunt Sarah. "Did you look at the Tintoretto?"

"Err, yeah. That was interesting, too." They looked at each other appraisingly waiting for the other to say something. Luke broke the silence. "I'm going to go upstairs to start on some homework."

"What did you think of your present?" shouted Aunt Sarah, but Luke was already closing his bedroom door. "I guess I'll get dinner ready then."

Whilst Aunt Sarah made herself busy preparing Luke's birthday meal, he was upstairs trying to come to terms with what had happened to him during his fight with Rick. He stared at himself in his mirror, willing the feeling back, but it wasn't happening. He closed his eyes and concentrated. Nothing. No rising feeling of power or confidence. Nothing at all. As he looked at his reflection, he noticed something vaguely different about himself. He seemed to be slightly bulkier than he had been this morning. Almost as if his chest and arms had been inflated somehow. Dismissing it as a trick of the light or that he was tired after a long, eventful day, Luke began to unpack his bag. His hand settled on the present Aunt Sarah had given him that morning. He looked at it properly for the first time. Wrapped in paper that was probably from the 1970s, it wasn't particularly big but had a weight to it that contradicted its size. Still not wanting to open it, Luke left it on his bedside table and made his way downstairs.

He was greeted by the smell of garlic and tomato sauce cooking away on the hob, with Aunt Sarah in her trademark apron shuffling around pots and pans.

"Dinner won't be too long. It's your favourite. Meatballs and garlic bread."

"Thanks, Aunt Sarah. I appreciate it."

As she continued her cooking, Aunt Sarah struck up a conversation. "So, did anything interesting happen today?"

Luke was struck with the feeling that Aunt Sarah knew something he didn't, but he remained neutral.

"Not really. Rick Tyler was up to his old tricks, but it was nothing I couldn't handle." Luke tried to sound as casual as possible.

"Oh, really? Last time you tried to handle it, didn't you end up with a bloody nose, no bus fare, a walk home in the rain and a cold that kept you off school for two days?"

Luke stared at her. "That's highly specific, but unfortunately accurate. This was different. Maybe I'm a little stronger these days."

Aunt Sarah assessed him. "Well, you do seem to have

filled out recently. In fact, it looks as though it's happened overnight. Curious. I hope you didn't hurt the poor boy?"

"Poor boy? You're kidding me, right? Have you seen him recently? He looks like the offspring of Jason Statham and The Rock."

"I have no idea who or what you're talking about, but I hope you realise that violence is never the answer."

"He's fine, I didn't hurt him," then under his breath, he muttered, "much."

"Good. I'm sure your disagreement could be sorted out with a good chat and a nice cup of tea. Now, then. Why don't you take a seat and I'll bring you some food?"

They made small talk during their meal until Luke noticed something on the table that he'd never really paid attention to before: a faded grey vase full of pink, yellow, and white flowers.

"Those look nice," he said. "What are they?"

"Oh, those? I picked them up today. Do you like them?"

"Well, they're flowers. I suppose they're alright."

"They've always been my favourite. I'm surprised you haven't noticed them before. They're snapdragons."

There was something in the way Aunt Sarah had said snapdragons that made Luke drop a meatball from his fork onto the plate, which plopped down and splattered sauce over the tablecloth.

"Snapdragons? Cool name," Luke said as he attempted to mop up some of the reddish-orange stains.

"Isn't it? They have two peak seasons of growth and do so in a variety of colours. Native to Europe, the United States and North Africa, their leaves and flowers have been utilised in poultices as it is believed they contain antiphlogistic properties."

Luke just stared at her.

"Anti-inflammatory, Luke. Don't they teach you anything in school?"

"Why 'dragon'?"

"Because the flower looks like the face of a dragon, naturally. They even open and close what could be called their mouth when squeezed. Wonderful things."

"Do you mean dragons or the flowers?"

"Why on earth would I mean dragons?"

Luke was just about to respond when Aunt Sarah continued. "Anyway, that's enough about my floral fascination. Tell me, did you like your present?"

"My present? Well, to tell you the truth, Aunt Sarah, I haven't got around to opening it yet. Sorry."

"Oh." She was disappointed. "No matter. Perhaps you can open it tomorrow morning at breakfast?"

"Sure. Let's do that. I am grateful you got me something, Aunt Sarah. It's just that..."

"I understand, Luke," interrupted Aunt Sarah. "Today was always going to be an unusual day."

Luke had the impression Aunt Sarah wanted to say more, but she stood up and began to clear the table, leaving Luke to stare at the flowers in front of him. A few moments later, she returned carrying a cake with 13 candles squished into it that threatened to set off the smoke alarm if he didn't do something about it quickly.

"Happy birthday, Luke. Why don't you blow out the candles and make a wish?"

Luke smiled at his aunt, closed his eyes and thought for a moment of two certain people and did just that.

6

That night, Luke's dreams were invaded by images of dragons, fire and a hundred-petrified Rick Tylers begging him for mercy. It was just after 1 am when the sound of something breaking downstairs woke him from his troubled sleep. Luke groggily got out of bed to investigate when other noises made him even more concerned. Glass shattered and there were definite sounds of a struggle between more than one person. He quickly picked up the nearest object he could find to use as a potential weapon. A rectangular rubber. Better than nothing, thought Luke.

He crept down the stairs and peered into the living room. A scene of destruction and chaos greeted him. The vase that had been holding the snapdragons was broken on the floor, lying next to the unconscious form of a man. The mirror over the fireplace had been smashed with several shards struggling to remain in their correct place whilst others were being crunched underfoot by the two people wrestling each other just in front of it.

The figures broke apart from their fighting to catch their

breath. One had his back to Luke and even though he was wearing a balaclava, Luke could tell that it was an extremely large man. After a brief pause, the man launched an astonishingly quick flurry of punches against the other person. Luke struggled to see what was happening as the actions were so fast. Clearly this man was an exceptionally skilled fighter. However, none of his blows found their mark as the second person expertly dodged and blocked them with a feline grace to their movements that made Luke's jaw drop in amazement.

Luke sidestepped to try and make out who the other person was. Through the blur of arms and kicks, he could see that it was a woman. A woman wearing black boots, black leggings, a black roll-neck jumper with black hair pulled back into a ponytail revealing a face that could've been found on the front of *Vogue* magazine. She looked like a ninja action hero and a sudden realisation hit Luke that he struggled to comprehend. For a moment, he didn't know what to say.

"Aunt Sarah?"

The attacker immediately turned in surprise at the sound of Luke's voice. As he did, Aunt Sarah wasted no time in launching a brutal kick between the man's legs. Luke winced and almost felt sorry for him as he watched the man whimper and fall to the floor.

"The very same. Why have you got a rubber? What were you going to do? Erase him?" She pointed at the man writhing on the floor as he gently sobbed. "Sorry you had to find out this way, Luke, but things are happening quickly. We need to leave, immediately."

Luke was frozen to the spot, mouth open and staring at this alternative version of his aunt. "But, what's happening?"

"Luke, there will be time for explanations later, but right

now, put some proper clothes on, grab whatever you think you'll need, and let's go. Now!" With that, she grabbed the man by his hair and delivered a swift judo chop to his neck that knocked him out.

A thoroughly confused Luke went back upstairs and robotically began to get dressed. He grabbed his phone, a charger, some clean pants and socks, and stuffed them into his rucksack. He was almost out of the door when something caught his eye. There, on his bedside table, was his birthday present from Aunt Sarah. He picked it up, put it in his bag, and went downstairs. As he arrived back in the living room, he found that Aunt Sarah had tied the two men together and gagged them. Both were still unconscious.

"Are they dead?" asked Luke.

"Dead? Of course not, but they'll have headaches that will hopefully last a week when they wake up."

"Who are they? How did you do this? They're so much bigger than you."

"Size is irrelevant, Luke, and I'm sorry I woke you up. I thought we had a bit more time, but clearly, I was wrong. They found you quicker than we expected."

"Wait, what? Me? They were looking for me? Why?"

"Because you're the Chosen One, Luke. You don't know it yet, but you're probably one of the best-kept secrets in history. Come on. I'll explain on the way."

"Where are we going?"

"You'll see."

The two of them walked to the garage and Luke made his way to the passenger side of Aunt Sarah's worn-out Nissan Micra, which was probably as old as Aunt Sarah herself. "Where are you going?" asked Aunt Sarah.

"I'm getting in your car."

"I think we need something with a bit more urgency, wouldn't you agree? You'd better stand back."

Pulling aside some dusty boxes, Aunt Sarah revealed a small keypad with symbols on it that Luke didn't recognise. She pressed some buttons and a low rumbling sound came from beneath their feet. Suddenly, the Micra and the ground beneath it began to rotate into an opening in the ground. Continuing its turn, the Micra gradually disappeared and was replaced by the sleekest, meanest-looking sports car Luke had ever seen.

"My list of questions about these events continues to grow."

"Get in, Luke. And mind your head."

Luke approached the passenger side.

"How do I open it? There aren't any handles."

"Just put your hand against the door."

"Oh, of course. Why didn't I think of that?"

Luke did so and, to his amazement, the door responded by noiselessly opening upwards to reveal an interior so luxurious and elegant, it looked like it belonged in a private jet. Luke slid into the low leather seat as Aunt Sarah loaded their bags into the tiny boot. As he closed the door, Aunt Sarah took her place in the driver's seat and started the engine, which gave a low growl, sounding eager to begin their journey. She looked across at Luke.

"Ready?"

"No."

"Good."

Aunt Sarah eased the car out of the garage, pressed a button which closed the door behind them and coolly began their journey into the early hours.

7

Neither of them spoke for about ten minutes as they headed out of their sleepy village to the busier roads that took them towards London.

"London?"

"Yes. At this time of night –"

"Morning," interrupted Luke.

"At this time of the morning, we should be there in about an hour."

"Where exactly?"

"Oh, let's not ruin the surprise just yet."

"So, are you going to explain what the hell's going on, or shall I try to work it out for myself?"

"I suppose you deserve an explanation. It's been an eventful few hours after all."

"Eventful? You think? I get woken up in the middle of the night –"

"Morning," quipped Aunt Sarah.

"Whatever. I get woken up to see you've changed from Nanny McPhee to Jane Bond overnight, two huge burglars, one whose head you've caved in and the other you well and truly Jackie Channed, lying unconscious in our home, Tony Stark's car hiding in my garage and I totally kicked Rick Tyler's butt yesterday which was incredibly satisfying, but ultimately baffling. What's going on?"

"You told me you didn't hurt Rick."

"And you told me a good chat and a nice cup of tea could sort out any disagreement. Did those blokes back at the house not like their brew?"

"Touché. Okay, perhaps I was slightly hypocritical in that instance. Regardless, I did what needed to be done."

"You told me I was the Chosen One. What are you on about?"

"Luke, it's your blood. Your blood is part of an ancient and unique bloodline that contains certain elements that give you particular abilities."

"What sort of abilities?"

"Well, I think you've already experienced one of them which put Rick Tyler in his place. It depends on the person, but if you're who we think you are, then your talents might well be limitless."

"And who do you think I am?"

"I feel we need some suitably dramatic music to accompany this dialogue, but no matter. You're the one, Luke. The one to save us all."

"From what? You're answering my questions with answers that lead to more questions. Do you even know how frustrating you're being?"

"And wasn't that a question?" She smiled at Luke, who remained stony-faced. "I'm sorry, Luke, but it's not me who should be telling you all this. The Master will explain better than I can."

"Oh, good. Now we're on to Doctor Who. So, who's the Master and what does he have to do with this?"

"You're about to find out. We're almost there."

Luke had been so engrossed in trying to make sense of their conversation, he hadn't been paying attention to where they were. Looking out of his window, he was surprised to see a very familiar sight. Rising majestically into the air and surrounded by four bronze lions, was Nelson's Column in the heart of London's Trafalgar Square. Behind it, and its own imposing sight, was The National Gallery.

"Really? Some people visit The National Gallery once in a few years. I come here twice in 24 hours."

"And all for a very good reason, Luke."

Aunt Sarah continued driving around the winding road that surrounded Trafalgar Square before turning sharply into a discreet alley that was barely big enough for her car to fit through. There were overflowing bins and rubbish strewn about the filthy street at the end of the pathway, and Luke had the uneasy feeling that several rodents were eyeing their car as they approached.

"You take me to all the best places, Aunt Sarah."

"Needs must, Luke. This place has served us well over the years."

"I assume Environmental Health doesn't come very often?"

As they reached the end of the alley, Aunt Sarah pressed a button to lower her window. Reaching out, she typed a series of numbers into a barely visible, grimy keypad which made part of an even filthier wall slide up to reveal a hidden entrance. The car suddenly lurched and was pulled sideways on a conveyor into the hidden doorway. Once fully inside, the wall slid back down into place and a series of lights switched on, providing a dim illumination.

"Full of surprises tonight, aren't you?" Luke observed.

"Just you wait, Luke."

No sooner had Aunt Sarah finished speaking when something else happened to the surrounding walls.

"Why are the walls moving up?" asked Luke.

"What? They're not, you wally. We're going down."

The car was descending at a steady pace, deeper into the strange building. After just a few seconds, it stopped and Aunt Sarah drove the car forward into an underground car park. It was empty except for a powerfully built, futuristic-looking motorbike.

"Oh, good. The Master's already here."

"That's his bike? Very cool."

Aunt Sarah parked the car next to the bike, and the two of them got out.

"Follow me," and she led the way through a door with a set of steps leading up. As they ascended, Luke fought off the urge to bombard Aunt Sarah with more questions, choosing to wait and hear what The Master had to say instead.

After climbing several floors, Aunt Sarah opened a door that led into a room Luke had been in earlier the previous day and, waiting there to greet them, was a familiar face. Standing next to Tintoretto's painting of St George and the dragon was Patrick.

8

"You!" exclaimed Luke.

"Me," responded Patrick.

"You're the Master?"

"I'm the Master."

"You?" repeated Luke.

"Me," repeated Patrick.

Luke looked to Aunt Sarah for confirmation.

"He's the Master," she confirmed.

"He's the Master?"

"I'm the Master," Patrick was enjoying himself.

There was an awkward silence.

"Is that really your motorbike in the car park?" asked Luke.

"Indeed. Do you like it? It's a custom-made Kawasaki Ninja H2/R. Capable of zero to 60 miles-per-hour in just two seconds, with a top speed of almost 300 miles an hour. I've made some modifications myself that I'm rather proud of. Perhaps you'd like to take her for a spin sometime?"

Luke couldn't believe what he was hearing. The motorbike he'd seen just didn't go with the tiny, elderly man standing before him.

"Um, okay. Not sure I'm old enough yet, but that would be great, Patrick. I mean, Master."

Patrick giggled. "Patrick is fine, Luke."

"Sure. Okay, Patrick. Thanks."

"Now then." Patrick clapped his hands together, shocking Luke back to reality. "I've taken the liberty of providing some refreshments for you both. You must be thirsty after the events of the last few hours."

Patrick had laid out a table with some biscuits and two steaming mugs of hot chocolate. Luke and Aunt Sarah took the drinks gratefully and Luke helped himself to a bourbon biscuit. Patrick reached into his inside jacket pocket and produced a silver hipflask which he took a healthy chug from.

"Bushmills?" asked Luke.

"Ah, so you were listening? How splendid. That's exactly what it is, dear boy."

"I hope you're not planning on driving after that?"

"I wouldn't dream of doing such a thing. I just so happen to be quite adept at distilling alcohol-free whisky. One of my many talents, if I say so myself."

Luke thought about asking more on this but added it to his list of questions for another time.

"So, Luke. Take a seat in front of this fine painting and all shall be revealed. You're due an explanation and I intend to provide you with one. I know that most teenagers have the attention span of an amnesic goldfish, so I'll do my utmost to condense this rather epic, filmic tale into a cine-matically friendly trailer version for you, hmm?"

Luke had understood little of that last sentence, so just

nodded politely whilst Aunt Sarah watched on with amusement.

"Are you sitting comfortably? Then I'll begin. Dragons were real."

Luke couldn't help but let loose a snort of laughter.

"Yes, that's a natural reaction, but it's true, dear boy. Dragons were very much alive and breathing fire all over the world. For aeons, dragons lived amongst us, terrorising entire countries and decimating their populations."

"So where did they come from?" asked Luke.

"We don't know for sure. Our best guess is they're related to dinosaurs and somehow survived the extinction event that wiped out their cousins all those years ago."

"So, really, it should just be called the event, right?" Luke couldn't resist teasing.

Patrick giggled. "Quite so. Regardless, dragons have been wreaking havoc for millennia and were on the verge of overtaking humans as the dominant species on Earth. They used to content themselves with living off livestock such as sheep and cows until they tired of those and turned their attention towards humans, but back around the fourth century, something threw the balance of power back in favour of us men."

"Ahem," coughed Aunt Sarah.

"And women, of course. Forgive me, Sarah."

"What happened?" Luke asked.

"Well, this is where our friend St George comes in. As I explained to you and your classmates yesterday, one dragon, in particular, was being a nuisance and gobbling up the residents of a small village in Italy. George slew the beast, the village converted to Christianity and George went on his merry way."

"I'm sensing there's a but coming."

"I don't like buts. Never have, never will. I will always choose however over buts."

Luke couldn't help but laugh out loud at this, much to Aunt Sarah's annoyance.

"Really, Luke? You're 13 now, not seven."

"Sorry."

Patrick remained oblivious. "Did I say something funny?"

"No, you didn't. Carry on," insisted Aunt Sarah.

"Very well. Where was I? Ah, yes. But, I mean, however –"

Aunt Sarah shot Luke a look, daring him to laugh. He didn't.

"There's so much more to the story. Whilst George and the dragon were fighting, something remarkable happened. As George dealt the grievous blow with his lance, the dragon managed to bite through his armour and one of its teeth pierced George's flesh."

"Ouch!" Luke winced.

"Ouch indeed. George removed the tooth and his wound was tended to by the princess he had just rescued. As I have already said, the king was so grateful to George for saving his daughter that the entire region converted to Christianity and George was heralded a hero. However, as George convalesced, his wound began to fester. He developed a fever and was in danger of losing his arm until something rather unusual happened."

"What was it?" Luke was now hanging on to Patrick's every word.

"One morning, his fever broke, and he completely recovered. His once rancid arm was fully healed and perfectly usable."

"But that's impossible!"

"You would think so, wouldn't you? Once the dragon had died, its remaining relatives that were scattered throughout the world also breathed their last. It would appear they were all connected somehow to George's dragon. George stayed with the villagers for a few weeks, helping them to build churches and to settle them into their new beliefs until he decided to move on. Contrary to legend, not only did he visit merry old England, he settled here, married here, had a family here and died here."

"And what about his super-healing powers?"

Patrick chuckled at this. "As it turned out, there was something in the dragon's bite, possibly from its saliva, that fused with George's blood and subsequently enhanced him considerably."

"Just like Spider-Man," enthused Luke.

"I suppose so. Hadn't thought of it that way."

"But how do you know about the saliva or tooth? Surely you'd need a sample?"

"We do have a sample," Patrick responded, "and don't call me Shirley!" Patrick couldn't help but laugh at this one, whereas Luke looked nonplussed. "Shirley, surely? No? Alas. Anyway, I say *we* have a sample, I should say *you*."

"What do you mean?"

Luke looked at Aunt Sarah, who was holding something in front of him. It was the gift she had given to Luke the previous morning.

"Open it," she said.

With tentative hands, Luke reached out and took the present. Carefully untying the bow and tearing the paper, a box was revealed. Lifting the lid, he couldn't help but gasp. Staring back at him and threaded with a leather band was, unmistakably, a large tooth.

9

"There you have it. The tooth shall set you free!" Patrick quipped.

"Err, thanks. Or should I say, fangs?"

Patrick clapped his hands together. "Oh, bravo, Luke. Bravo!"

"Put it on, Luke." Aunt Sarah said.

Luke did so and immediately felt a warm sensation flood his body, like how he had felt when Rick Tyler confronted him. It calmed and excited him at the same time. The tooth seemed to heat up against his throat and, looking at it, Luke was sure its colour had changed to appear ever so slightly whiter. Patrick and Aunt Sarah shared a knowing look.

"That tooth is now bound to you, Luke. It is yours and can only be removed from your neck voluntarily," said Patrick.

"Why me?" asked Luke.

"I'll get to that, dear boy. There's more to the story. The night George's fever broke, he appeared to be at death's door. He was rambling incoherently, and his temperature was dangerously high when, suddenly, he lay completely still and began to speak in a perfectly calm voice, quite contrary to how he had been moments before. The princess, remember she was nursing him, wrote George's words on a piece of parchment. Would you like to hear what was said?"

"Of course," Luke nodded eagerly.

"Sarah, would you do the honours?"

"The strength of the dragon flows through my veins, for I and my bloodline, that power shall remain. The last of their kind has now been slain, but malevolence in other forms shall rise again. We are the guardians of blood and tooth, keeping our secret to protect the truth. There shall come a time when evil grows and our hopes lay with the one now chose. On the day of his 13th year of birth, he shall then discover his true worth. For in this boy all our hopes rest. To live in dark or light will be his test. They will come to vanquish us all. United we must stand, or else we shall fall. In the place of the stones when the moon is red, the final challenge awaits where one will be dead."

Deafening silence greeted Aunt Sarah's words.

"You see, Luke," Patrick broke the quietness. "You are the boy from St George's prophecy. You share his bloodline, as do I and your Aunt Sarah. For centuries, many of your ancestors have used their powers for good, fighting evil and keeping our way of life as safe as possible. The tooth has been kept hidden for centuries, regularly changing its home to keep those that would steal it, guessing. For not all that share the blood of St George walk on the side of good. There are those that walk in the dark and have been seeking the tooth to further their desires. When the blood and tooth are brought together, they combine to give the wearer unimaginable strength and power. Thankfully, so far, those that have handled the tooth and are descendants of St George have walked in the light. We have chosen our Guardians well. Your great-grandfather being one of them. But you, Luke. Your powers will be even greater due to you being the subject of the prophecy."

"But, surely this prophecy applies to any kid that has George's blood and hits 13?" Luke protested.

"A valid point, Luke. However, all the signs point to you. Your parents were both of George's bloodline –"

"Gross." Luke screwed up his face at this. "Isn't that weird?"

"Not at all. Many years had passed and George's ancestors were quite a scattered bunch."

"And what's the deal with the end of that prophecy? Red moon, challenges and being dead. If I am who you say I am, are you telling me I might actually die?"

"Alas, this is the gravity of the situation we find ourselves in, young Luke. We believe there is a procedure of some sort that needs to take place during a total lunar eclipse. As I'm sure you're aware, during a total lunar eclipse, the moon appears to be red because it is illuminated by light that has passed through Earth's atmosphere and has been bent back towards the moon by refraction."

"Yeah, I totally knew that." Luke glanced at Aunt Sarah, who rolled her eyes.

"However, you will not be alone. I am here to help you as is your Aunt Sarah and there will be others to ensure that your death doesn't happen."

"Right. You'll forgive me if I don't jump for joy at that."

"Tell me something; what did you see when you were studying the Tintoretto painting?"

"How did you know I saw something?"

"I was listening to you and your *Star Wars* obsessed friend."

"I saw writing on George's lance, but I couldn't read it."

"Interesting. Why don't you take another look?"

Luke stood up and walked over to the painting. Squinting slightly, he lowered his head until it was level with the lance. There, in the same silver writing but no longer faded, was the text. Luke could feel the warmth of the tooth once again.

"It's a different language. I think it's Latin. Wait, I *know* it's Latin. 'Lumen eorum qui in tenebris sunt'."

Patrick couldn't contain his joy. "Yes, Luke! It means, 'Be the light for those in the dark'. You see? Nobody but the Chosen One could have read that. Tintoretto was a gifted guardian, and this was a perfect way to help find the Chosen One. Hiding in plain sight and all that. He wrote this hundreds of years ago and shared his doing so in his diary. Oh, I've been waiting for years to find out what the message was."

"Luke," it was Aunt Sarah who spoke. "As Patrick was saying, with parents like yours, we all had our suspicions it would be you. From what you've told me about what's happened to you over the last day or so, watching how you reacted to wearing the tooth and now being able to read the hidden message, can't you see it, too?"

"I imagine strange things have been happening to you, eh Luke?"

"You could say that, Patrick. It wasn't exactly a typical birthday."

"Quite so. Rather a lot to digest, hmm?"

"That prophecy. Who's coming to vanquish us all?"

"Ah, yes. Well, I believe that specifically refers to something that began over 80 years ago, in Germany. As I'm sure you know, the Germans have tried unsuccessfully to take over the world twice. World War I and World War II. Adolf Hitler was obsessed with many things, including supernatural powers. He authorised numerous hunts for religious artefacts, including The Holy Grail, The Ark of the Covenant and even a search for the bones of Jesus Christ. He also financed a search for that very tooth you wear around your neck."

Luke's hand instinctively went to his new gift.

"In 1940, he captured one of our finest Guardians. Your great-grandfather, John Stevens. John was one of the bravest men I ever knew and he went to his grave protecting St George's legacy and the great-grandson he never knew he was going to have."

Luke mulled this over, surprised at how emotional he felt about a man he never knew.

"Patrick, just how old are you?" Luke couldn't help but ask.

Patrick's smile seemed to grow even wider as he answered.

"My dear boy, I'm older than I used to be and younger than I'm going to be."

"Well, that's cleared that up," sighed Luke.

"Getting back to your question, young Luke, even though the Germans lost the war, a small group of Nazis escaped justice and lived to fight another day. I believe it's those same Nazis that have strengthened their numbers and will come at us attempting to claim the tooth for their own. If they succeed, they might take over the world after all. I fear the time is nigh for there to be one final battle between good and evil and if evil prevails, darkness will reign and Hitler may just get his thousand-year Reich even if he isn't around to witness it."

"What do you mean? I know I've heard that word before, but what's a Reich?" Luke asked.

"A Reich means regime or empire. The First Reich was

the medieval Holy Roman Empire which lasted until 1806 and the Second Reich included the German Empire from 1871 to 1918," explained Patrick.

"1918? That's when the First World War ended, isn't it?" Luke asked.

"That's right. Hitler's Third Reich began in 1933 and he envisaged a Thousand-Year Reich. Thankfully, because of millions of brave men such as your great-grandfather and millions of equally brave women, that didn't happen. But if your tooth were to fall into the wrong hands, the world could be catapulted into tyranny and disaster. The consequences for our way of life are too terrible to contemplate."

Luke took a moment to digest Patrick's words.

"How are we going to stop them? I mean, there's only three of us. Aunt Sarah's alright, but with these new powers I'm like Bambi learning how to walk, I'm only 13 years old and you're about 106. No offence."

Patrick gave his usual giggle. "None taken, and you need not worry. Yes, you're young, but I have no doubt that you shall rise to the challenges before you. Also, we shall regroup with other Guardians as soon as we can to bolster our numbers. Now, if you're fully refreshed, I believe it's time for us to be on the move. If the Nazis tracked you down to your house, they can probably track you here, too."

"How right you are, Herr Kelly."

All three turned to see who the unknown voice belonged to. Walking into the room with an air of arrogance was a tall, blonde man with cold blue eyes dressed in a crisp black military uniform. He was leading four other men, all carrying pistols and all wearing a badge on their lapel showing the ultimate symbol of evil, the swastika.

10

As the man took up a position in front of Patrick, Aunt Sarah and Luke, the others stayed just behind him, weapons raised and pointing at the trio.

"Patrick, it is good to see you again after so long," spoke the man with a slight German accent.

"Sebastian. Alas, it hasn't been long enough," Patrick responded, making no attempt to keep the contempt from his voice.

"Sarah, you are looking as beautiful as ever."

"Why don't you come closer so my fist can thank you properly, Sebastian?"

Luke couldn't help but chuckle at this, which made the man turn to face him.

"And this must be the one and only Luke Stevens. Luke, it is a pleasure to make your acquaintance. I have heard so much about you."

Luke stayed silent, eyeing Sebastian with as much hatred as he could show. Sebastian returned a patronising smile as his eyes found the leather band around Luke's neck.

"You have something that I want, Luke. You will give it to me and maybe you and your friends will get out of this alive."

"I don't know what you're talking about," Luke responded defiantly.

"The tooth, Luke. I want the tooth."

"I am telling you the tooth." This one made Patrick smile.

"I have never been a fan of British humour and I am losing my patience," continued Sebastian. "Around your neck is a tooth belonging to the dragon that was killed by St George. Take it off and hand it to me."

"You didn't say 'please'."

There was a pause as the two stared at each other.

"Please. And I will not ask again."

Luke looked at Aunt Sarah and Patrick. Both smiled encouragingly at him and he felt reassured by their presence.

"Look, Sebastian, is it? Under normal circumstances, seeing a group of Nazis pointing guns at me and my Aunt Sarah would be really weird. However, I'm just going to add this to my ever-increasing 'strange things to happen to Luke since he reached 13' list. I've had a bizarre few hours and I don't appreciate you barging in here like Billy Big Balls, with your goons and your guns threatening my family and friend. I'd appreciate it if you would, in fact, bugger off."

The two stared at each other. It was Patrick who broke the silence.

"Who's Billy Big Balls?"

Nobody answered him.

"I see you have your great-grandfather's spirit, Luke. He was brave, too. But his bravery also got him killed."

Luke's jaw clenched as Sebastian spoke of his great-grandfather.

"Don't you dare talk about my great-grandfather. You didn't know him."

"Oh, you are quite right. I did not know him. But my great-grandfather did. My great-grandfather was one of the last people to see him alive."

"Sebastian, please," interrupted Patrick. "He doesn't know these details and he shouldn't be hearing them from you first."

"You have not told him? Tut tut, Patrick. Surely the boy deserves to know how he died?"

"What are you talking about? What's going on?" demanded Luke.

"It is very simple, Luke. My great-grandfather killed your great-grandfather," Sebastian said coldly.

Luke let this information sink in. He looked over at Patrick, who met his gaze with a sorrowful look.

"Who exactly are you?" Luke asked.

"My name is Hitler. Sebastian Hitler."

The silence that greeted this seemed to last an eternity.

"That's ridiculous," said Luke, "Hitler didn't have any children."

"And how would you know?" Sebastian snapped. "All my life, I have had to justify my genealogy. I am tired of non-believers."

"I don't understand," Luke answered.

"My great-grandmother had a relationship with Adolf Hitler during World War I whilst Hitler was a soldier fighting in France. She subsequently gave birth to a boy, my grandfather."

Luke digested this new information and struggled to keep the disbelief from his face. He looked at Patrick and Aunt Sarah.

"Is this true?" he asked.

It was Aunt Sarah that responded.

"It might be."

"Be careful, Fräulein," warned Sebastian.

"It might be," Aunt Sarah repeated. "You don't have any proof."

Sebastian exploded. "Proof! You ask me for proof? My great-grandmother telling my grandfather on her deathbed is proof. Why would she lie? Hitler himself admitted to their relationship."

Luke looked at Patrick.

"Patrick? Is it true?"

Patrick took a furtive glance at Sebastian, who was barely concealing his rage. He chose his words carefully.

"It's certainly possible, young Luke."

Luke considered this as the group appraised one another. Sebastian calmed himself and spoke first.

"Now that we are all familiar with each other, let us get back to the matter at hand. The tooth, if you will."

Luke's hand reached up to feel the centuries-old tooth. Its warmth calmed and comforted him.

"No," he stated. "You can't have it, you Nazi prat."

"What?" asked Sebastian.

"Sorry. I meant, nein. Du kannst es nicht haben, du Nazi-trottel."

Aunt Sarah looked at Luke in surprise.

"I didn't know you could speak German."

"Neither did I," answered Luke. "Guess that's another perk of being the Chosen One."

"Enough!" bellowed Sebastian. "I asked you nicely, but

you have decided to go the same way as your great-grandfather. This ends now. Kill them!"

As Sebastian issued his order and his colleagues steadied themselves to fire their guns, all the lights above them suddenly went out, plunging the room into darkness. Luke didn't hesitate and reached out for Aunt Sarah and Patrick, finding them both quickly.

"Stay low and follow me," Luke shouted urgently. He quickly pulled them both towards the hidden doorway they had used to enter earlier on. The sound of gunshots echoed through the large room, and the hiss of bullets whizzing past them threatened to deafen them. But Luke maintained his composure. He assumed that was thanks to the tooth and his new abilities. Indeed, it took him a moment to realise that even though he was surrounded by darkness, he could still see clearly. His vision had taken on a mystical, greenish tinge, like night-vision, and he smiled ruefully at yet another new ability. In between the sound of the guns, Sebastian was desperately trying to make himself heard.

"Stop! We need to hear them. Stop shooting, fools!"

The guns fell silent and Sebastian and his men strained to hear any sound made by Luke, Aunt Sarah or Patrick, but it was too late. The three had already made their escape and were running furiously back up the stairs towards the car park.

11

"Well, that was slightly more eventful than most trips to the National Gallery," joked Luke.

"How on earth did you get us out of there so quickly, Luke?" asked Aunt Sarah.

"Night-vision eyes, obviously."

"Oh, how wonderful, Luke. You're going to be full of surprises," chuckled Patrick.

"That's all well and good, but why don't we concentrate on getting out of here alive first?"

The three of them descended the stairs quickly and made their way into the car park. Aunt Sarah's car and Patrick's motorbike were still there, but so too was a large man pointing a gun at them. They froze in their tracks.

"Let me handle this," Luke said, stepping forward. "I don't know who you are, but I know what you want. You can't have it. If you try to take it, I will hurt you. Now stand aside or feel my wrath."

The man couldn't help but smile. "Wrath? Most impressive, Chosen One, but I'm not here for your tooth." He spoke with a deep, American accent. The man lowered his gun.

"Oh. Then what do you want?"

Aunt Sarah and Patrick moved past Luke and rushed to embrace the stranger. The three exchanged some words that Luke couldn't hear. Luke couldn't help but notice Aunt Sarah held on to the man's hand a little longer than normal. He was well over six feet tall and powerfully built. His handsome face had a coldness to it, yet also a reassuring confidence that showed experience and courage.

"Err, hello!" shouted Luke. "Could somebody explain who the new guy is and why you're not running away from him?"

It was Patrick that answered. "Luke, this is Marcus Carter, one of the Guardians I was talking about earlier. Thank goodness you came when you did, Carter. It was getting a little hairy up there."

"Yeah, I noticed. I'd hacked into the security cameras of the Gallery on my cell phone when I was on my way to you, just in case. Turns out it was a sensible thing to do. Looks like I cut the power just in time, but how the heck did you get out so quickly?"

"All thanks to young Luke, here. It would seem he's full of surprises and his powers are growing exponentially."

"As nice as it is to meet you, Marcus, don't you think we should get ourselves and St George's dragon's tooth away from the Nazis that want to kill us? Now there's a sentence I never thought I'd say," said Luke.

"Please, call me Carter."

"Luke's quite right. Sarah, take Luke. Carter, you're with me," said Patrick.

"How will the two of you fit on that bike?" asked Luke.

"Remember, I've made some modifications. We shall

both be quite comfortable. Sarah, head for the Mount and we'll reconvene there."

"Will do. Come on, Luke." Aunt Sarah gave a quick smile towards Carter, who returned it with a wink.

As Luke and Aunt Sarah ran towards their car, he looked back over his shoulder to see Patrick fiddling with what looked like a mobile phone. Somehow, the motorbike's seat seemed to grow, becoming longer and wider so that it could easily accommodate both men's frames. Luke couldn't help but be impressed.

As they climbed into the car, they heard the aggressive roar of Patrick's bike starting up and the two vehicles drove into the lift system together. It quickly began to ascend. Seeing Patrick's tiny body straddling the huge motorbike with Carter's enormous bulk overshadowing him from behind was one of the most bizarre and humorous sights Luke had ever seen.

"You know, on any other day that would seem unusual."

The lift reached the top and slid them back out into the alleyway. Patrick led the way onto the main roads of London. They'd only been driving for a few seconds when a loud crack made Luke turn. As he did, something pinged off the back windscreen.

"What the hell was that?" shouted Luke.

"A bullet. Don't worry, she's armoured. But we've got company."

Aunt Sarah was right. As Luke continued to look behind him, he could make out two motorbikes and a car in pursuit. He couldn't tell who was riding the bikes, but the unmistakable figure of Sebastian was driving the car. The Nazis were chasing them.

"This Sebastian's a real jerk," said Luke.

"You don't know the half of it. Hold tight. This is going to get rough."

Aunt Sarah pressed her foot down harder on the accelerator, and the car shot forward at an astonishing speed. Because it was still early, there was hardly any traffic and only a handful of pedestrians. Luke could see the looks of confusion on their faces as they tried to process what they were seeing. After all, it wasn't every day you saw motorbikes and cars involved in a high-speed chase.

Aunt Sarah typed a few numbers into a keypad next to the steering wheel. The sound of a telephone ringing filled the car, which was promptly answered by Patrick.

"Sarah, this is turning out to be quite a night!"

"We need to split up. We're going to head towards Waterloo Bridge and take the plunge. Hopefully, Sebastian will follow us because of Luke."

Luke looked at her curiously.

"An excellent idea," Patrick responded. *"We'll take the more scenic route to lose our pursuers. No doubt Carter is itching to try some of the new weapons I have on board."*

"You're not wrong there!" Carter chuckled.

"Carter, if you don't mind, could you work some of your magic on the CCTV cameras in the area? I think it's best if we try to stay as anonymous as possible. How are you doing, young Luke?"

"Oh, I'm fine. Just a little worried my English homework isn't going to be handed in on time."

"Really?"

"No! I still don't understand what's going on and I've got Hitler's great-grandson trying to put a bullet in me. How do you think I'm doing?"

On cue, another bullet pinged behind them.

"Point taken. Well, you're in the more than capable hands of

your Aunt Sarah, so just sit back and enjoy the ride. We'll see you soon."

The call ended.

"Enjoy the ride? Is he for real?" Luke asked.

"He's quite a character."

"You can say that again. Will they be alright?"

"They should be. Patrick's a wily one and a lot tougher than he looks. Besides, he's with Carter. He'll look after him."

"Yeah, what's the deal with Carter? I saw how you two looked at each other."

"Really, Luke? Don't you think there should be more important things on your mind right now?"

Aunt Sarah shot Luke a glance, which made him back off. She turned the steering wheel to the right as Patrick continued straight on. As hoped for, the two motorbikes followed Patrick whilst Sebastian's car kept its sights firmly on Aunt Sarah and Luke. A couple more bullets smacked off the armoured car.

"So, I assume you have a plan?" asked Luke.

"Of course. We just need to hold them off until we get to Waterloo Bridge and we'll be fine. No bullets can penetrate this car. I'd be worried if they had a bazooka though."

Luke's face had paled.

"What's wrong?" Aunt Sarah asked.

"They've got a bazooka."

Aunt Sarah used her mirrors to see behind her. Hanging out of the car's sunroof was one of Sebastian's soldiers, armed with a rocket launcher and attempting to steady himself before firing.

"Interesting. This could work to our advantage."

She steered the car expertly through the quiet London roads, weaving across both lanes to throw off the soldier's aim. As she did this, Aunt Sarah also pressed a button which was next to the steering wheel.

"Let's go old-school on these guys. Oil-slick coming up."

Seconds later, Luke could see what looked like black water falling from the back of their car, covering the road behind them. Sebastian tried to avoid driving through it, but there was too much oil to avoid. The slick liquid coated the car's tyres and caused them to spin uncontrollably. Or so Aunt Sarah had hoped. Sebastian somehow kept the car from crashing into the surrounding buildings. He clipped a couple of parked cars, which slowed him down, but he wasn't out of the chase. Aunt Sarah had put a fair amount of distance between them, although they weren't out of the woods yet. Luckily, Waterloo Bridge was just up ahead. Aunt Sarah performed a perfectly executed handbrake turn and made her way onto the bridge. The bridge ran straight for about 370 metres. Aunt Sarah accelerated but didn't put her foot all the way down. Subsequently, they hadn't gone too far when Sebastian's car came screeching around the corner and began to close the gap between them.

"They're behind us and that bloke with the bazooka's back!" exclaimed Luke.

"Perfect. You need to hold on, Luke. This is going to get weird."

"Oh, now you tell me."

When Aunt Sarah's car was about halfway across the bridge, the soldier holding the bazooka was finally able to get his shot off. The rocket whooshed out of the launcher with a thin trail of grey smoke and began its journey towards the back of their car. Just as it was about to hit, Aunt Sarah yanked on the steering wheel and pressed another button near the dashboard. The missile slammed into the road just underneath the car and with a tremendous boom a huge fireball catapulted it into the air and over the side of the bridge where it plummeted towards the murky depths of the Thames. There was no time for Luke to scream as the car smashed into the water with an almighty splash and quickly began to sink beneath the shadowy surface.

12

W hilst Luke and Aunt Sarah were busy trying to escape Sebastian, Patrick and Carter had the two soldiers on motorbikes to contend with. After watching Aunt Sarah move off to the right, Patrick continued going straight ahead, choosing a different path out of London. He then veered sharply to the left, aiming for the neon lights of Piccadilly Circus and the many side roads surrounding it.

"I hope you know where you're going, Patrick," shouted Carter over the roar of the motorbike's engine.

"Of course, dear boy. Now, if you'll look at either side of you, you might see a small indentation in the paintwork. Do look closely because it's quite easy to miss. If you can't see it, run your finger over the paintwork and you should feel a tiny mark, much like braille."

Carter was disappointed when he couldn't see anything. Using his fingers, he ran them along either side of the bike, finding both marks at the same time.

"Found them!" he yelled.

"Splendid. Now, simply push your thumbs into them."

Carter did so and instantly, two compartments extended outwards, both filled with small weapons. There were guns, but also metallic discs, like ice hockey pucks.

"Woah," said an impressed Carter.

As the motorbike zigzagged its way through the streets of London, the two pursuers were doing their best to keep up with Patrick and had little time to draw their own weapons. Needing both hands to control their bikes, this was not a problem for them. The soldier nearest Patrick and Carter was about 60 yards behind them and used his thumbs to manipulate some control panels by the motorbike's handlebars. Two small, thin machine guns were revealed on either side of the front headlight. Using his fingers to operate a handle that housed the trigger, he began to strafe bullets towards his target.

"Incoming, Patrick!"

"Well, what are you waiting for, dear boy? Fire at will, or whatever his name is!"

"But I don't know what these do!"

"You'll get the hang of it, I've no doubt. With the guns, point and shoot. With the discs, push the button and throw."

"That's what I love about you, your in-depth instructions. What could go wrong?"

Carter grabbed one of the guns, noting how it seemed to thrum with energy once he had gripped it.

"Keep her steady whilst I turn around."

Carter positioned himself so that he had his back to Patrick and was facing his pursuers. Using his thighs to grip the seat and steady himself, he brought the gun up, took aim, and pulled the trigger. The gun spat out a small, electric-blue pellet that struck the soldier directly on his chest and remained there. However, rather than falling off his bike wounded, nothing happened. The soldier knew something had hit him, but carried on with his pursuit.

"Patrick? What's happening? Something hit him, but he's still coming!"

"Wait for it, my dear boy, but look away when the light goes out."

No sooner had Patrick finished speaking when the pellet began to pulse with intense light. The soldier was looking at it in confusion. The pulsing stopped for a split second before a brilliant white light flashed from within. The soldier began convulsing and was unable to move his hands from the handlebars of the bike. His body was rigid and unable to control his balance or movement. He steered the bike into a lamp post, where he finally let go and landed on the floor in a crumpled heap, still twitching. The bike's front wheel had come off in the collision and was bouncing further down the road. The second soldier was still giving chase, glancing at his fallen colleague as he passed him by.

Although Carter had followed Patrick's instructions and looked away at the right time, his eyes were still a little blurry from the explosion of light. He blinked rapidly to get his sight back to normal as quickly as possible.

"What the hell was that?"

"That, my boy, was my Pelletricity gun. I've been waiting to see it in action and I'd say that field-test was a resounding success!"

"Pelletricity?"

"Yes. Quite simply, it fires a small pellet that contains a charge of electricity to cause neuromuscular incapacitation, like a Taser. Once activated by contact, the electricity also ignites a mixture of magnesium and potassium nitrate which causes the explosion of light which temporarily blinds. Like a stun grenade. If our friend survived the crash, he'll have a headache for several hours and his vision will be compromised for longer, hopefully."

"Are you joking? How on earth did you manage that?"

"I never joke about my work," a surprisingly serious Patrick chided. "But perhaps now isn't the best time to discuss the ins and outs of my pyrotechnical marvel? After all, there is one more Nazi on a motorbike after us."

Sure enough, the remaining soldier was still giving chase, keeping a cautious distance after seeing the bizarre takedown of his comrade. Wary of what might be fired in his direction, he weaved as much as possible along the road, hoping to make himself a hard target to hit.

Patrick's knowledge of London's streets had seen them making several turns, and they now headed along Embankment with the spectacular sight of the London Eye next to them, across the river. Behind them, Big Ben towered majestically.

Because this was a wide, straighter road, the soldier gained confidence and began advancing quickly on Patrick and Carter.

"As much as I enjoy seeing the many wonders of this magnificent city, I think it's time we left it behind. Wouldn't you agree? Be a good chap and let our German friend have a closer look at one of those discs. Once you've pushed the button, you'll have five seconds to throw it. Or is it three? I was never particularly good with numbers."

Carter was incredulous.

"Well, which is it? Five or three?"

"Five. I'm sure it's five."

"What happens if you're wrong?"

"Oh, don't worry. I'm rarely wrong."

"That isn't very reassuring, Patrick."

Carter couldn't see Patrick's smiling face.

As the soldier's motorbike advanced, the shooting started up again. Bullets chipped the tarmac near Patrick's bike and struck some of the parked cars on either side of the road. Carter pressed the button and began a count in his head. He needed to time his throw perfectly so the disc could do whatever the disc was going to do. When he had reached three, Carter threw the metallic object towards the Nazi. His aim was off, though, and the object whistled past the motorbike's wheels and exploded about 10 meters behind it. Carter heard a muffled 'whump' and what looked like a grey liquid shot into the air where the explosion had happened. The soldier continued, hope renewed that he might finally catch his prey.

"I missed!"

"If at first you don't succeed, do better!"

Taking another disc, Carter steadied himself for another shot. Just as he was about to push the button, he quickly picked up another one.

"Say hello to my little friends," he muttered.

Pressing both buttons, he waited a couple of seconds before throwing one and then the other, hoping that if one missed, another would hit.

The soldier saw both coming and did his best to avoid them, but because Carter had thrown them the way he had, it was impossible. Narrowly missing the first disc, the second exploded underneath his bike as he travelled over it. The thick, grey liquid flew out from the disc like a geyser, coating the bike's wheels and most of the soldier too. Within moments, the bike suddenly stopped moving, and the soldier was catapulted from his seat and began skidding down the road, tearing his clothes. When he eventually came to a stop, the barely conscious soldier found he couldn't move his arms or legs. The grey liquid had become a dense sludge, making movement virtually impossible. He rocked from side to side, desperately trying to get to his feet.

"He's gone, Patrick. What on earth was that stuff?"

"Why, that was my Binding Ultra-glue Mine. It'll take a pneumatic drill to get that stuff off him."

There was a pause as Carter considered this.

"You realise that abbreviates as BUM?"

Patrick hadn't thought of this.

"Oh. That's slightly embarrassing. Well, no matter. It is what it is, and it's my Binding Ultra-glue Mine."

"I guess you could say you were sticking with that name?" Carter quipped as he once again faced forwards on his seat.

"Bravo," Patrick chuckled. "Now, what say you and I put some distance between us and our enemies, hmm?"

No sooner had Patrick finished speaking when they heard an explosion in the distance behind them. Looking back, Carter could see a fireball coming from the direction of Waterloo Bridge.

"Oh no. Sarah!" he whispered.

As Patrick and Carter continued away from London, Sebastian's car pulled up to where Aunt Sarah and Luke had last been seen. Peering over the edge of the bridge towards the water, he could just make out bubbles rising to the surface, which rippled from the impact of the car. He continued to stare downwards, his face devoid of emotion. He turned away to examine the still smoking crater in the road before him. As the sirens of the emergency services sounded in the distance, Sebastian received an incoming message on his mobile phone. After reading it, he allowed a small smile to flash across his face before returning to his car.

13

The moment the car hit the water and began to sink, Aunt Sarah began feverishly typing numbers into the keypad on the dashboard.

"Are you still with me, Luke?" she asked.

"We're sinking. What are we going to do?"

"Do you know who made this car?"

"I'm guessing it wasn't Henry Ford."

"It was Patrick. He, as you know, is something of a technical wizard. We're perfectly safe in here for a couple of days like this if need be."

"That's easy for you to say. You don't need the toilet."

Aunt Sarah glanced over at him.

"Don't worry, I was joking."

The car suddenly stopped its descent and levelled off. Aunt Sarah pushed the steering wheel towards the dashboard and the car responded by moving forward.

"Tell me you didn't just do that?" Luke asked.

The car continued onwards, with Aunt Sarah at the controls.

"Yep. You currently find yourself in one of Patrick's Subcarines."

"I bet he thought of that name, right?"

"Of course."

Remarkably, the car had indeed transformed some of its parts to make it suitable for an aquatic adventure. The wheels had retracted into the car and were now sealed. A powerful jet was helping to propel it forwards. Strong headlights just about penetrated the filthy water of the Thames, but they could only see about five metres in front of them.

"Welcome to your private tour of the River Thames," began Aunt Sarah. "On your left, you will see hardly anything, but coming up on your right is a shopping trolley with what looks like an old boot inside it."

"How fast can this go?"

"Pretty fast. We can't go too quickly here because it's so murky, but once we're out into the North Sea, we can open her up a bit."

"Do you think Patrick and Carter are okay?"

"I think they're absolutely fine, Luke. It'll take more than Sebastian and a few goons to stop them."

"That missile didn't hit us, did it? You did something to the car."

"Very good, Luke. I did indeed. As you can see, Patrick has installed several unusual features here, and I used one of them to help get us out of that rather tricky situation. I blew the back tyres."

"You what?"

"Exactly what I said. It's something I've never had to make use of before, but it certainly came through for us today. I quickly over-inflated the back tyres, which caused the rear of the car to rise. As they burst, they helped to propel the car into the air. Combined with the explosion caused by the rocket and my twisting the steering wheel, we were blown over the edge of Waterloo Bridge to exactly where I wanted us to go."

"How did you know that was going to work?"

"I didn't, but it was worth a try."

"That's quite a gamble. Do you think it fooled Sebastian?"

"Doubtful. But it's certainly bought us some time and I'm pretty sure he doesn't know where we're going next."

"Where are we going next? What's the Mount?"

"Perhaps the question shouldn't be 'what', but 'where'."

Luke waited for Aunt Sarah to expand on this. She didn't.

"You're infuriating," he said. "Fine. Where's the Mount?"

"What do you know about Cornwall, Luke?"

"Cornwall?" he thought for a moment. "Pasties, beaches and pirates. Oh, and scones. Or is it scones?"

"Slightly stereotypical and generic, but that's probably a standard response. The Mount belongs to a family called Knight, and we shall be going to their house. They also happen to be fellow Guardians."

"And they live in Cornwall?"

"That's right. Near Penzance."

"See? *The Pirates of Penzance*, right? Isn't that some kind of musical?"

"It's nice to know you have some culture within you. Yes, it's an opera written by W. S. Gilbert and Arthur Sullivan in 1879. Interestingly enough, there's a very famous song featured in it called 'the Major-General's Song' which –"

"I'm going to stop you there," interrupted Luke. "The words 'interestingly' and 'opera' do not belong in the same sentence."

"Rude. When you're older, you'll appreciate the finer things in life."

They shared silence as Aunt Sarah navigated the Subcarine through the Thames, picking up speed as they headed towards the North Sea. Luke's mind was awash with all the things that had happened to him over the last few hours. How quickly he'd gone from being an ordinary 12-year-old to a 13-year-old with special abilities and the fate of the world resting on his shoulders. Luke's eyes began to get heavy. As he was drifting off to sleep, he suddenly had a flashback to his parent's funeral and the two men he had seen standing aloof from the other mourners. He had a feeling they were Patrick and Carter, but sleep wrapped its warm embrace around him bringing an end to those thoughts.

Aunt Sarah watched him for a few moments, a look of love and pity etched on her face. She sighed and continued driving.

It was early morning with the sun just beginning to rise from its slumber as the Subcarine slowed down on its approach to their destination, St Michael's Mount. If they were above the water, they would have seen the spectacular sight of a stone castle sitting atop a tiny island. Owned by the same family for over 400 years and although some of them still live there, tourists are allowed to visit and explore certain parts of it.

"Luke, you need to wake up. We're here."

As Luke began to stir, Aunt Sarah guided the vehicle towards an underground entrance. The tide was still in, which hid their arrival.

"Did I doze off?" Luke asked.

"No, you usually have drool hanging from your lip."

Luke wiped the offending line away with his sleeve. The

Subcarine glided closer to what looked like an enormous pile of rocks. As it did, to Luke's astonishment, part of the rock face disappeared and a doorway large enough for them to fit through was revealed.

"I'm not even going to ask," said Luke.

"They know we're here. I imagine Patrick let them know to expect us and they also have many underwater cameras to aid their security. We're lucky the tide's still in. A car emerging from the sea and driving towards the harbour might have looked a tad suspicious to anyone watching from the mainland."

"You think?"

The Subcarine was swallowed by the hole in the wall which slowly closed itself up once they were safely beyond it. Aunt Sarah allowed the natural movement of the water to carry them into what appeared to be a large glass or Perspex box. There was a panel in front of them and on either side of their doors, and as they settled, a fourth and final panel rose behind them to seal them in.

"Well, if I wasn't claustrophobic before, I certainly am now," said Luke.

The box began to rise with the grinding of gears and the water made a whooshing sound around them. They continued upward for several seconds until they arrived at what looked like the world's most lavish garage. There were cars ranging from sports cars and luxurious saloons to off-roaders and jeeps, motorbikes of varying style and even three or four small but expensive-looking boats.

"I take it these Knights have a bit of cash floating around then?" Luke asked .

The box was lowered onto a concrete platform, where it stopped moving. There was a drop around the perimeter of the platform, which was raised about a foot higher than the floor surrounding it. From the ceiling, a winch was lowered, which hooked onto a metal loop on the top of the Perspex box. There was a crunching sound and suddenly, all but the floor of the box was lifted into the air above the Subcarine. The seawater that had collected in the box was instantly released into the void beneath the platform.

"Mind your step, Luke."

Aunt Sarah opened her door and carefully stepped outside onto the platform. Luke did the same, and they jumped over the gap and onto the concrete floor. As the pair of them got their bearings, they heard voices approaching. They turned towards the sound and saw the familiar faces of Patrick and Carter along with a man of similar age to Carter that Luke didn't recognise.

"Ah, Sarah and Luke. We've been expecting you. Well, I have, but poor Carter here has been desperately worried ever since he saw that explosion on Waterloo Bridge. I told him it would all be part of your plan and he needn't worry, but he's been fretting ever since," explained Patrick.

"Why didn't you just call us?" asked Luke.

"A valid question, young Luke," answered Patrick, "but water, especially the murky water of the Thames, wreaks havoc on our communications and it did also occur to me that Sebastian might have somehow found a way to listen in to our conversations so I wanted to avoid any unnecessary contact."

"It wouldn't have been unnecessary," Carter sounded annoyed.

"Carter, we've been through this and I stand by my original assessment."

There was an awkward silence as Carter glowered at Patrick and then turned a more gentle gaze upon Sarah, who seemed to blush ever so slightly as she smiled at him.

"Anyway, Luke, I'd like to introduce you to Maximillian Knight, a fellow Guardian and the current owner of the magnificent St Michael's Mount."

"Please, call me Max."

Max stepped forward and offered Luke his hand to shake. Luke did so and found that it was clammy and limp. Not a hand he wanted to hold on to for too long.

"I've heard so much about you. Have to say, you're not quite what I was expecting." Max looked Luke up and down with what appeared to be disdain.

"Oh. How so?"

"Well, you're the Chosen One, are you not?"

"So I've been told."

"I was just wondering why it was you that was chosen. You don't look particularly special."

Luke didn't know what to say, but Aunt Sarah answered for him.

"I think you'll find, Max, that Luke is full of surprises. He saved our lives back in London."

"How nice to see you again, Sarah, and may I say how lovely you're looking? For your age." Aunt Sarah was about to respond when Max continued, glancing at Luke. "Did he save your life? Or was that Carter? Hmm?"

Before anyone could answer, Max continued. "Anyway, shall we head upstairs? I don't know about any of you, but I'm famished. Breakfast should be served imminently."

Max led the way upstairs, towards the tantalising smell of fried food. Luke hadn't realised just how hungry he was, and his mouth began to water. As they moved through similar-looking corridors, Luke used the time to have a better look at Max. He was just under 6 feet tall with greying brown hair neatly parted on the side. A thin scar running from his top lip across to his right ear gave the impression that he was permanently sneering. He walked with confidence and held his chin up, which made him look down on people. Although he was wearing jeans, his other clothes were more formal. Highly polished black shoes click-clacked along the stone floor, whilst he wore a red and black cravat underneath an expensive shirt with a matching handkerchief poking out of the pocket of his brown corduroy jacket. Luke could hear him droning on about the history of the Mount and how disappointed he was that the public could still visit during certain times of the year.

"They come here in their droves, hoping to glimpse us. I suppose it's good for business and community relations to let the plebs in, but goodness me, some of them are awful. No class, no manners, just a bunch of selfie-taking oiks. Do you know, I'm supposed to talk to them now and then? Honestly, can you believe that? Ghastly affair. I don't enjoy getting too close to them if I can help it. Still, if the fools want to give me cash for having a look at how the other half lives, who am I to stop them?"

Luke wasn't sure he liked Maximillian Knight.

"Are you sure he's a Guardian?" Luke asked Aunt Sarah.

"Sadly, yes. And, believe it or not, a very good one, too. The Knight family are some of the oldest Guardians of all. I will admit, he's an acquired taste."

"What happened to his face?"

"That is a story for another time."

Finally, they arrived in front of a large, solid wooden door. Max opened it, and the others followed. An extravagant crystal chandelier hung overhead in the centre of the room above a table that had room for at least 20 people. Several oil paintings hung on three of the walls. Some were of people, including Max, others of the Mount, with one or two showing battles with dragons. The last wall, which was in front of Luke, was home to an enormous window, taking up nearly the entire width of the wall. Luke walked over to inspect the view. It was stunning. The sun was still rising and looked like it was being born from the sea itself. The waves were gently crashing against the base of the Mount, causing white, foamy water to rise and fall quickly. It was a spectacularly beautiful sight.

"Not bad, eh?" Max stood next to Luke.

"It's amazing."

"Yes, I suppose for someone like you, coming from that tiny home of yours, this must all seem rather daunting. Well, you needn't worry. Perhaps some of this castle's charm will rub off on you." With that, he clapped Luke hard on the back and strode to the table.

"Idiot," Luke muttered after him.

Luke had been so taken with the view that he'd not noticed what was on the table when he'd entered. On silver serving trays were piles of bacon and mounds of eggs. Scrambled, fried, poached and boiled. Toast, butter, cereal, croissants and many hot and cold drinks, too. As Luke took a seat as far from Max as possible, he noticed a woman flitting in between the party, helping them with their food.

"That's it, Patrick, the eggs were boiled for three minutes and 52 seconds exactly. Just how you like them. I've even cut you some soldiers as well. Here you are." She loaded Patrick's plate with strips of toast that all remarkably looked the exact same size and shape. "And you, Carter. Three fried eggs, three rashers of bacon, three sausages, three buttered slices of bread and topped off with baked beans. There you are, dear." She put the plate in front of Carter, whose eyes lit up. "Sarah, how lovely to see you. You're looking more beautiful than ever."

Max let out a derisive snort that he turned into a cough.

Luke clocked it, but Aunt Sarah was too busy beaming at this new addition to the party.

"Felicity, it's so nice to see you, too."

"Here's your breakfast. A croissant, Greek yoghurt and orange juice, freshly squeezed, of course."

"You're a lifesaver, Felicity. Thank you."

"And who might this handsome young man be?" Felicity said, turning to Luke. "I'll tell you who you are."

"Okay..." said Luke.

"You're Luke Stevens." Felicity clapped her hands excitedly as she said this.

"That's right. It's nice to meet you, Mrs...?"

"Knight, dear. I'm Maxi's wife, Felicity. Oh, I've heard so much about you and I'm thrilled to be meeting the Chosen One!"

"Thanks, Felicity. Thanks for the food, too."

"Oh, you're welcome, dear. Just doing my bit. Us Guardians must stick together. Let me get you some food, dear."

In a flash, she was gone and heaping food onto Luke's plate. Felicity was rather short, slim and incredibly light on her feet. She reminded Luke of a fairy from a Disney film. Her blonde hair was bobbed, which she wore with a headband. She was dressed similarly to her husband, including a matching red and black cravat. When she walked, it looked like she was gliding. Luke couldn't help but smile as he watched her.

"Are you sure *she's* a Guardian?" Luke asked Aunt Sarah.

"She's more of an honorary Guardian and doesn't do much fieldwork, if you know what I mean. Felicity's more of an administrator. She and Max fell in love a long time ago and he insisted on bringing her into the fold."

"Here you are, Luke, dear," Felicity returned and placed Luke's food in front of him.

"Thanks. This is quite a home you have here."

"Thank you. Yes, we're incredibly lucky to have it. There's so much history and character to her, but as you saw downstairs, she also has her surprises and no shortage of secrets." She gave Luke a playful wink as she said this.

As Luke ate his food and Felicity spoke to Aunt Sarah, he couldn't help but notice that Max would glance at him now and then. He wasn't making eye contact, though. He was looking at the leather band around his neck that held the dragon's tooth. Luke thought he'd play a little game with Max. The next time he felt Max's eyes on him, he reached into his shirt and gripped the tooth. Just as he was about to pull the tooth out, a glass of orange juice spilt onto his plate.

"Oh, I'm so sorry, Luke," said Felicity. "How awfully clumsy of me." She grabbed some napkins and began to dab away at the liquid that had formed a colourful swimming pool around Luke's sausages.

As Luke helped her clean up, his eyes were drawn to the huge window.

"What's that?" he asked.

Everyone turned to follow Luke's gaze.

"What's what?" answered Patrick.

"In the sky. That cloud."

It was a clear day with only the sun on display.

"What on earth are you on about, boy? There's only the sky, sun and seagulls out there. Honestly, Patrick. Are you sure this is the right boy?" scoffed Max.

"I'm telling you, there's something out there." Luke got up from his chair and moved towards the window. He put his hand up to the glass and squinted into the distance.

The others gathered around him, all scanning the skies

for a hint of what Luke claimed he could see. It was Carter that spoke first.

"He's right. Look over there, to the left."

True enough, in the distance was what looked like a small black cloud. Only this cloud was getting bigger and bigger the closer it came.

"I don't like this," said Luke as he began to edge backwards.

"I'm with Luke," agreed Carter. "Something's not right."

With astonishing speed, the cloud was getting closer and closer to the Mount.

Luke continued to stare, concentrating on the dark mass. Luke's blood ran cold.

"They're drones! Everybody take cover, now!" he shouted.

As the group quickly moved away from the window to seek shelter, several of the drones began to smash into the glass, which, amazingly, didn't break. Those drones ended up falling into the sea below.

"I told you she had her secrets," said Felicity. "That glass is bulletproof. It'll take more than a few pesky drones to get through it."

Luke ran to the door to open it, but it was locked.

"The door's locked? Why is it locked? Who's got the key?" he shouted.

"I do," answered Felicity. She put her hand in her pocket but looked confused. "It's not there. I don't have it! What are we going to do?" she began to panic, her breaths coming fast.

"Carter, Max, help me with this." Luke made his way to the table they had just been sitting at and began to lift it. Max was about to protest about being told what to do by a child, but Carter gave him a look that stifled his complaints.

Even though it was incredibly heavy, Luke raised it slightly off the ground and, with the other's help, they were able to flip it over, which provided a slight barrier against the drones should they need it.

As numerous drones continued peppering the window by flying directly into it, others began to hover in clusters about 50 metres away and fired bullets. It wasn't long before tiny cracks began to appear in the glass.

"Felicity, I know you've already said this place has her secrets, but I don't suppose there are any others you'd like to share with us right now?" asked Luke.

Felicity was on the verge of hysteria. "What? I'm not sure. I don't know. What are we going to do?"

Luke hadn't noticed, but behind him and crouched near the door was Patrick, who was busy fiddling with the door handle.

"Patrick, whatever it is you're doing, please do it quickly," said Luke.

"Panic not, young Luke. Being able to pick locks has opened up a lot of doors for me."

Nobody laughed. Instead, everyone took cover behind the table. The cracks began to spread wider and quicker until, finally, the glass shattered with an almighty crash and blew inwards, spraying shards all over the room. The drones' guns stopped and silence descended.

"Is everyone okay?" whispered Luke.

Nobody said they weren't which Luke took as a good sign, although Felicity was crying. Luke risked raising his head above the table to see what was happening outside. His eyes were drawn to one drone that was slightly larger than the others, but further back. Luke's eyes widened as the drone fired a missile directly towards them.

14

As soon as the missile was fired, Patrick finished picking the lock and had swung the door open.

"Everyone, quick! Leave now!" he shouted.

The group didn't need to be told twice and ran towards the open door as fast as they could. Luke noticed it was Aunt Sarah that helped Felicity through, rather than Max, who was the first to leave. So much for chivalry, thought Luke. Carter was the last out and slammed the door shut behind him just as the rocket blasted into the table where they had been moments before. Although the thick stone walls of the castle provided some shelter, the explosion was still enough to hurt their ears and knock them off balance. Dust fell from the ceiling as they staggered through the corridor.

"We have to get to the chapel. It's our only chance of getting off the island," shouted Max above the noise of the remaining drones, which were still firing weapons into the castle.

Max took them up several flights of stairs followed by Patrick, Aunt Sarah, Felicity, Luke and Carter bringing up the rear.

"Why the chapel?" asked Luke. "And how did Sebastian know we were here?"

"We don't know that it's Sebastian," answered Max. "We shouldn't jump to conclusions."

"Yeah, right. Bit of a coincidence, don't you think?"

"It's certainly a curious set of circumstances," said Patrick.

"I don't believe in coincidences," grumbled Aunt Sarah and shooting Max an accusatory look.

"I can feel your eyes on me, Sarah. I hope you're not suggesting what I think you're suggesting?"

"How many people knew we were coming here, Max? He found us at the Gallery and he's found us here. How do you explain that?" spat Aunt Sarah.

"I can't," Max responded, "and I don't appreciate you accusing me of being a traitor here in my own home, especially after I welcomed you and saved your skins."

"May I suggest we leave this bickering behind us and get to the chapel whilst we're still relatively unscathed? We can examine the whys and wherefores once we are safe," Patrick interjected.

They continued climbing stairs and running down corridors until they were all struggling for breath. Luke was amazed that Patrick was keeping pace with them. He even looked like he was enjoying himself.

"Patrick, why are you smirking?" Luke asked.

"Isn't it a wonderful time to be alive? I find there's nothing like a good chase, with bullets and missiles whizzing around and exploding to remind one that life is worth living. And we've had two in one day! I haven't had this much fun in years."

"I'm seriously worried about you."

As they reached what appeared to be a dead-end, Max ripped a tapestry from the wall to reveal a hidden doorway.

"Everyone, listen to me. Behind this door is a courtyard with about a 50-metre run to the chapel. We don't know what's waiting for us outside, but we need to assume there are more drones. Therefore, move fast and don't stop. I'll lead us into the chapel where we should be safer."

He turned to face the doorway and put his left hand flat against it.

"This is going to open the door. It'll stay open for as long as people keep moving through it. Don't hesitate, or it will close and you'll be stuck here," Max explained.

"Max, why didn't I know about this?" asked Felicity, sounding hurt.

Max ignored her. With a grinding noise, the door moved outwards and began to slide to the side, opening up.

"Watch your step," advised Max.

Max sprinted off towards the chapel, with the others following. The courtyard was exposed and several drones that had been scouting the area caught sight of them and began to move into position.

"Quick! Keep moving. They're coming!" yelled Max.

They sprinted across the courtyard and up a short set of steps to the entrance of the chapel. Just as Max shouldered open the unlocked door, bullets from the drones began to strafe the courtyard, causing stone chips to fly off in all directions. The rounds were getting closer and closer to Carter, who was once again at the back of the group. Just as it looked like the guns were going to find their mark, Carter dived through the doorway, where Patrick was waiting to slam the door shut behind him.

"Thanks," said Carter.

"It's this way," said Max as he barged past his wife

towards the altar at the back of the building. Intermittent thumps came from the chapel's door as bullets and the drones themselves bashed into it.

"We must hurry." Max went behind the altar, lifted the faded cloth that was covering it, and once again pressed his hand against one of the flat stones underneath it. A keypad emerged, into which he quickly typed a series of numbers. The keypad then retracted back into the stone which itself slid back to reveal a hidden staircase descending into a tunnel. This time, Max let the others go first. Discreetly, he pulled out his mobile phone, pressed a few numbers, and then pocketed the device once again. But not before Luke had glanced back to see what he was doing. Max made sure the cloth was back in its correct place and followed the others down into the darkness. As the steps finished, he looked back to see the stone sliding back into place.

"Everything alright?" Luke asked.

"Apart from my house being destroyed, everything's rosy, Luke," he responded as he shouldered past him.

"How do you get back up to the top?" questioned Luke.

"Not that it's any of your business, boy, but there are hidden sensors that respond to my palm-print."

"Fancy."

The group gathered at the bottom of the steps. Their eyes had adjusted slightly to the darkness, but it was still hard to see. For a moment, all that could be heard was their breathing, with Felicity's being rapid and louder than the others.

"Carter, Sarah. If you have a mobile phone, I suggest you use the torch option now, like me," Max whispered.

"All this technology, yet you couldn't get LED lights for down here?" quipped Luke.

"Quiet, boy," snapped Max.

One by one, three lights illuminated, making everyone squint as the brightness enveloped them. Luke took in his surroundings, noting that the phone Max brought out was different from the one he had just seen him with. The tunnel they were in was a little over six feet high. Carter had to stoop slightly. It continued downwards at an angle which Luke assumed took them under the sea. The walls were ancient and the smell of damp was strong. The silence was interrupted by the sound of Felicity sobbing. Max appeared to walk towards his wife to offer comfort, but walked straight past her and down the tunnel. It was left to Aunt Sarah to console Felicity instead.

"Hey, don't worry. We'll be fine now," Aunt Sarah soothed.

"I don't understand. How did those things find us and what are we doing down here?" Felicity struggled to catch her breath. "Max. What is this place? Why didn't I know about it?"

Max stopped walking and turned to face the others. He looked furious.

"It's always prudent to have a backup plan, and this escape route has been in my family for generations. It's several hundred years old. We'll be travelling directly under the sea so expect your feet to get a little wet. As to why I didn't tell you?" he warily looked at his wife and then the others. "Well, I'll explain that when we're somewhere more private. We need to move."

They continued into the tunnel, which was just about wide enough for them to walk in pairs. Luke walked next to Patrick.

"Patrick? Can I ask you something?"

"You just did. What is it, dear boy?"

Luke deliberately slowed his pace to be further away from Max.

"How well do you know Max?"

"Max? I've known him for most of his life, so almost forty years."

"Do you trust him?"

"I'd trust him with my life."

"It's just – well, it's probably nothing, but I thought I saw him acting suspiciously a moment ago and he's not exactly the friendliest person."

"Apart from his arrogance, conceitedness, stubbornness, rudeness and snobbery, I think you'll find he's quite a nice chap. You don't need to worry, Luke. The poor man has just seen his ancestral home blown to smithereens and we're all on edge right now, so I'm sure what you saw was just his way of dealing with things."

"If you say so."

Just in front of Luke and Patrick walked Aunt Sarah and Carter.

"How are you holding up, kiddo?"

"I'm fine, thanks. Worried about Luke and all this new information he's having to deal with."

"He's a strong and smart boy. He's going to be fine."

"Is he though? Sebastian and the Nazis are hunting us down far too easily. Something's wrong, but I can't quite put my finger on it."

"I agree," said Carter. "We have little choice but to go with it, for now. Let's see where Max takes us next and we can reassess."

"I'm glad you're here with us. With me." Aunt Sarah looked up at Carter, smiling.

"Sarah, there's nowhere else I'd rather be. Well, Paris or Rome might be a better alternative to being hunched over in an ancient underground tunnel where the walls might cave in at any moment unleashing the full might of the North Sea on us whilst at the same time a group of murderous Nazi thugs are after us."

"The life we lead, hey?"

"Sarah, I promise I won't let anything happen to Luke."

The two looked deep into each other's eyes.

"I know, Carter. I know. Thank you."

In front of Aunt Sarah and Carter were Felicity and Max. The two were talking in hushed whispers, eager to avoid being heard by the others. Felicity was still visibly upset and sobbed as she spoke.

"I don't understand. You're my husband. Why didn't you tell me about this place?"

"We're allowed some secrets from each other, surely?"

"What's that supposed to mean? What else are you keeping from me, Maxi?"

Max scowled at her. "Pull yourself together, will you? You're embarrassing me and yourself."

The further they walked, the more water was accumulating at their feet, with small drips seeping through the walls of the tunnel.

"This is a magnificent feat of engineering, Max," called Patrick. "Do you know who built it?"

"I believe it was created by the first of the Knights to come into possession of the Mount in the 17th century to discreetly aid some of their more, ah, morally questionable activities."

"You're from a family of criminals? Bet you keep that quiet," laughed Luke.

"Certainly not, and I'd ask you to hold your tongue when it comes to my family, boy. It was a different world back then, and the Knight family were pioneers. Certain items, including several medicinal ingredients, were illegal in England. My ancestors made sure the poor had access to them in their time of need."

"For a price, though, right?" Luke retorted.

"Of course. It was a business, after all."

"Not exactly Robin Hood?"

At this, Max stopped and slowly turned to face Luke.

"You know nothing of my family. Nothing. Perhaps your aunt here will fill you in on our history. That's if she can tear herself away from gazing at Carter like a love-sick puppy."

"Watch it, Max," hissed Aunt Sarah.

"I'd listen to the lady if I were you, Max," said Carter.

"Lady? She might be a woman, but she certainly isn't a lady."

At this, Carter and Sarah both lunged for Max. Luke and Felicity quickly grabbed and held back Carter and Max, respectively, whilst Patrick attempted to placate Aunt Sarah. When Patrick spoke, it was with a tone of voice Luke hadn't heard before. Surprisingly forceful, it was authoritative and commanding.

"Enough! All of you. Carter and Sarah, take a moment. Max, you're being more of a pompous ass than usual. If you're not careful, I'll let Carter loose on you. I believe we currently have enough problems to deal with from external forces without having to deal with internal battles as well. We all need to calm down and figure a way out of this mess."

The tension was palpable as the group took a collective breath. Carter and Aunt Sarah walked a few metres away whilst Max shook himself free of Felicity to compose himself.

"Max, where exactly are you taking us?" asked Patrick.

Max shot a look towards Aunt Sarah and Carter before steadying himself to speak.

"This tunnel will eventually lead us to a small field, which is near a car park. In the car park are a couple of Guardian cars that we can use to put some distance between us and whoever is chasing us."

"Sebastian," said Luke.

"Perhaps," answered Max.

"Well, let's not waste any more time with this pointless bickering and get to it, shall we?" said Patrick.

He took Max by the arm and guided him onwards. The others followed, with Aunt Sarah and Carter moving in sullen silence. After a few minutes, they came across stone steps.

"Ah, marvellous. The end is nigh," said Patrick.

Max led the way up. Once again, he placed his hand on what appeared to be stone, and a keypad appeared. Luke observed Max as he typed in a brief sequence of numbers. The keypad retracted, and the stone slid back to allow the group to leave the tunnel. As they exited, the stone slid back into place, camouflaged with grass to retake its position, hidden in plain sight. As Max had said, Luke and the Guardians found themselves in a field surrounded by trees.

"So, what now?" asked Luke.

"Now, Luke, you will give me what I want," a familiar and unwelcome voice responded.

From out of the trees behind them came a group of men, all dressed in the same dark, camouflaged military uniform and all holding guns. Leading them was Sebastian Hitler.

15

"Guten Morgen, Guardians. How wonderful to see so many of you together on this fine day," Sebastian said as he stopped several metres in front of them, his soldiers holding a line just behind him.

"How did you find us?" asked Aunt Sarah.

"Oh, that is not for me to say, Fräulein."

"I know," said Luke. "It was this posh prat," he pointed at Max. "I saw him messaging on his phone just before we entered the tunnel. Then, when we needed light, he used a different phone. I knew from the start you weren't to be trusted and now look what you've done!"

"That can't be," said Patrick. "Max, tell me this isn't true."

Everybody was looking at Max.

"It's not what you think. Yes, I had two phones with me, but I wasn't messaging anyone." Max revealed both phones to show them.

Carter swung an enormous fist into Max's face, making him drop the phones and knocking him to the ground.

"How could you, Max? They're Nazis. Evil in its worst form. After everything the Guardians have been through over the centuries and you sell us out now?" Carter screamed at Max, who was struggling to his feet.

A gunshot echoed through the silence.

"Enough!" ordered Sebastian, who had fired his pistol into the air.

Max struggled back to his feet as his nose and lip dripped blood onto the grass. The other Guardians looked at him with disgust.

All except one.

"So that's where my phone was. Bravo, Maxi," Felicity said, slowly clapping her hands. "When did you know it was me?"

"I've had my suspicions for a while. I just needed proof." Max didn't hide the contempt from his voice.

"Well, I have to say, I'm relieved. All those years of being married to such an insufferable snob have not been my idea of fun. You're quite honestly the most obnoxious man I've ever met and the worst part is, you don't see it yourself. That hideous, superior outlook you have has truly blinded you to the reality of the world around you."

"Superior outlook? Isn't that the Nazi way?" hissed Max.

"Oh, I'm not doing this for the Nazis. They can have their power. I'm here for the money and I aim to make a lot of it."

"We have money. Why do you need more?"

"No, Max. *You* have money. I don't have any and I'm sick of it."

Felicity stormed towards Max.

"I want to give you something to remember me by, you pretentious fool."

She slapped Max's cheek, leaving a red welt across it, and walked towards Sebastian.

"Was any of it real?" whimpered Max.

Felicity slowly faced him and noticed he had tears running down his face.

"Do you remember what you said to me when we got engaged in Venice? About your love for me and how much I meant to you? It meant nothing to me then, and it means nothing to me now." She turned her back once again. "Stay safe, Maxi, stay safe."

Guilt and pity threatened to overtake Luke.

"Max?" Luke said. "I owe you an apology."

"Quiet, boy. Your words are meaningless." Max sounded broken.

"Wow. Guess I'll save my pity for someone else then."

"As amusing as it has been to watch your heart break, Maximillian, it is time for us to be on our way," smirked Sebastian. He clicked his fingers and immediately four shots rang out from the guns behind him.

Luke instinctively flinched, but didn't appear to be hit. Confused, he looked around to see Patrick, Carter, Max and Aunt Sarah drop to the ground and lie still. Sebastian was laughing.

"How does it feel, Chosen One? To see those you love, die? I wanted you to watch them fall, knowing they died at my hand."

Luke's rage was building. He stared at Sebastian, allowing his anger and pain to consume him. Sebastian looked worried and quickly clicked his fingers again. This time, just one gun was fired. Luke was hit in his neck and was immediately propelled backwards. He landed in an awkward heap with his back to Sebastian. But he didn't feel any pain. He gingerly reached up to his neck and felt something loose hanging from it. He carefully pulled it out and saw that it was a tranquillizer dart. Touching the skin around where the dart had penetrated, it felt tough, almost like scales. Luke's mind whirled as he realised Sebastian hadn't killed his friends at all. He'd sedated them instead and, somehow, the dart hadn't been able to fully penetrate Luke's skin.

Sebastian walked over to Luke and found the tooth around his neck. He reached out his hand to grasp it, but just as he was about to touch the tooth, a scorching heat sliced across his hand causing him to retract it immediately.

"Curious. Pick them up and prepare them for transport," ordered Sebastian, rubbing his injured hand.

Luke played dead for now, his hope renewed. He was going to think of a plan, rescue his friends, and stop Sebastian.

"Come, Felicity. Soon, the tooth shall be mine and the New World Order can begin."

Without looking back, Felicity took Sebastian's hand and left the Guardians, including her husband, for the Nazis.

Luke was bundled into the back of a military truck along with Max and secured to a stretcher by his wrists and feet. Four of Sebastian's soldiers were with them. Patrick, Aunt Sarah and Carter were loaded into a different vehicle, this one with five soldiers. Sebastian and Felicity were chauffeured in an elegant saloon car which took the lead as they left Penzance, followed by Patrick's truck, with Luke's bringing up the rear.

Luke forced himself to breathe deeply and to remain as calm as possible. He was desperately trying to think of an escape plan. The soldiers were talking to each other in German and making jokes about the Guardians, unaware that Luke understood every word they were saying. When one of them said something rude about Aunt Sarah and the others laughed, Luke couldn't help but become incensed. He allowed the anger surging through his veins to increase whilst, at the same time, attempting to control his emotions. Slowly opening his eyes, he could see the four soldiers in front of him and used his peripheral vision to note that Max was to his right, bound the same way he was. Luke knew what he had to do, and that he had to do it fast. Allowing the energy to swell inside him, Luke waited for a raucous amount of laughter and then leapt into action.

Snapping both the restraints holding him in place as though they were twigs, Luke sat bolt upright and threw himself off the bed. Before the soldiers knew what had happened, Luke had swung his right fist into the face of the nearest guard, knocking him unconscious. He immediately followed that up with a left hook that took care of the soldier opposite and instantly shot out his left leg in a perfect kick that connected with the third soldier's jaw, throwing his head back and making his eyes roll as he collapsed. The fourth soldier had snapped out of his temporary daze and was reaching for his gun just as Luke clamped a hand around his mouth and used his other arm to twist the soldier's body and slam him into the floor of the truck. Although winded, the soldier fought back and punched Luke on his nose. It didn't hurt as much as it should have, but Luke could feel the warmth of his blood trickling down one nostril, which made him even more determined to end this quickly. Using an arm and his body weight to pin the soldier down, Luke manoeuvred his other arm into the soldier's neck and throat, restricting the supply of oxygen to his brain. Applying pressure, gradually the soldier's fight became weaker until his flailing stopped completely. He'd live, but would be very sore when he came around.

Luke took a moment to control his heart rate and to take stock of the situation. Once again, he felt weak and tired. He took a moment to sit down and recoup some of his energy.

Looking at the bodies of the four Nazis on the floor around him, he couldn't help but laugh. First Rick Tyler and now highly trained soldiers from one of the most feared armies in the world. Recovering, he searched the soldiers for the keys to the restraints, took them off properly and did the same for Max. He also took anything that might be of use later, including weapons, ammunition and a pair of radios. A first aid box was also raided, just in case. He put everything into a backpack that was lying under the seats the soldiers had been sitting on.

About ten minutes had passed since their journey had begun. Luke didn't know whether the guards in the front of the truck would check on their prisoners or not, but he had to assume they would at some point, so time was of the essence. First, he had to figure out how to get himself and the unconscious Max out of the moving truck.

16

L uckily for Luke, the rear of the truck was covered in canvas. Luke had taken one of the soldier's knives, so slicing a hole big enough for him and Max would not be a problem. He began to cut away, the efficiency of the knife making light work of it. Once an escape passage big enough for both of them to fit through had been sliced, Luke was relieved to see that they were still travelling through relatively quiet roads and hadn't reached any kind of motorway yet. There were a few cars scattered around, including one about twenty metres behind Luke's truck. Nothing he could do about that. Hoisting Max's dead weight onto his back, he waited until the truck slowed down enough for him to risk jumping out. He didn't have to wait long. As the truck rounded a tight bend, it slowed just enough for Luke to hang his legs over the back of the truck and to allow himself to fall onto the road, with Max over his shoulders. It was a rough landing and Luke stumbled forwards. Max was thrown onto the road in front of him, straight into the path of the oncoming car. The driver slammed his foot onto the brake pedal, stopping just inches from Max's head. As Luke once again lifted Max onto his shoulders, the elderly driver of the car wound down his window and stuck his head out to speak to Luke.

"Are you alright, son? What's going on?"

Luke thought fast, and inspiration hit him. He raised a finger to his lips.

"Shh. Training exercise. I've got to get my friend back to base without the other members of the squad catching us."

"Oh. Right you are. Do you want a lift anywhere? I'm ex-army myself."

Luke couldn't believe his luck.

"Yeah, I would actually. Thanks, that would be great."

"Hop in, son. Let's get you back before you're found out."

Luke opened the back door of the car and put Max into a seat, fixing his seatbelt in place. He then sat in the front passenger seat. The truck had increased its speed as it disappeared around the corner. The old man looked curiously at Max and then at Luke.

"Is he alright? Why is he not speaking?"

"Oh." Luke lowered his voice conspiratorially. "He takes these training exercises very seriously. Likes to stay in character, you know like how some of those actors do? He won't answer you no matter how hard you try to talk to him."

"Gotcha. Good for him. Where are we headed to?"

"You'll need to turn the car around. Towards St Michael's Mount. There's a car park with a field near it. Do you know it?"

"Reckon I do. Right you are."

As the man drove, he made small talk with Luke. Turns out he'd joined the army as a teenager, but had left after a few years because of his regular issues with authority and many run-ins with superior officers. When he spoke, it was with a strong Cornish accent.

"Bleddy morons in charge when I was in the game. Poshos straight out of Eton or Oxford or wherever else they slide in from. I couldn't take being ordered about by a bunch of soft, rich pillocks that would sooner have a manicure than get their hands dirty. The last straw was when one of the bleddy idiots was promoted over me due to him being the son of a colonel. I didn't like that, so I decked him. My feet didn't touch the ground after that. So, I came back down here to become a fisherman. Been doing that these last 40 years. Good, honest work. Bless my soul, where are my manners? I'm Eddie."

"Luke. That's Max."

Before too long, the car was pulling into the car park.

"Reckon this is the place. That field you're looking for is just over there, past the ticket machine."

Luke exited the car, put on his backpack, and went to get Max. Once again, up Max went onto Luke's shoulders. Eddie got out of the car to shake Luke's hand.

"Before you go, aren't you a little young for the army?"

"I'm older than I look, Eddie. I find it lulls my enemies into a false sense of security."

"Reckon it probably does. Well, best of luck to you, son. Don't take any guff from anyone and you'll do alright."

"Cheers, Eddie. I appreciate that. You've saved me more than I can tell you. Look after yourself."

As Eddie drove off, Luke smiled at his good fortune. Quickly moving off towards the field, he found a quiet spot well away from the car park, laid Max onto the ground, and rummaged around in his backpack for the first aid kit. He needed Max awake and functioning if he was to rescue Carter, Patrick and Aunt Sarah.

There was nothing in the medical bag that would help wake Max up, so he devoured an energy bar that he found and made a decision. He would have to carry Max back to St Michael's Mount and hope he could remember the way to Patrick's Subcarine.

It took a bit of searching, but Luke found the hidden entrance to the tunnel and dragged Max along to it. He held Max's hand flat against the grass and moved it around, hoping to find the sensor that would activate the hidden keypad. After a few moments, a small patch of earth where Max's hand was seemed to sink into the ground ever so slightly under the extra pressure caused by Luke. Up popped the security pad, showing its metallic interface. There were several squares, including 10 numbers from zero through to nine. Luke closed his eyes and concentrated. He cast his mind back to when he and the Guardians had exited the tunnel. Luke had been watching Max closely ever since he saw him with two phones and had deliberately angled himself so that he could see Max at the keypad when he typed in the code. Confident that it had been a four-digit sequence he'd used, Luke did his best to remember where his fingers had been when entering the numbers and how they'd moved.

The first two attempts didn't work and Luke was worrying he might be locked out. He remained calm, focused on his breathing, and rested his palm against the keypad. Concentrating, his other hand instinctively reached up to the dragon's tooth to hold it. Luke could feel a warmth coming from some of the squares on the keypad. Directing his energy to the hand on the keypad, he felt the heat coming from it and intuitively pressed the four hottest numbers. The keypad retracted, and the hidden entrance slid aside, revealing the steps leading into the tunnel. Breathing a sigh of relief, Luke quickly gathered his things, heaved Max up onto his shoulders again, and climbed down the steps to begin his journey back to St Michael's Mount.

Even with his newly revealed strength, Luke still had to stop and rest several times along the tunnel. His night vision had kicked in, enabling him to see almost perfectly in the dark space, so he did not need a torch. Finally, they reached the end, and Luke once again used Max's hand and ran it across the stone slab at the top of the steps. He did this slowly to make sure he didn't miss the hidden sensor. Sure enough, Max's hand activated it and the keypad revealed itself. Luke promptly typed in the same four digits hoping the code was the same. It was, and the slab slid away, allowing them to climb out.

Luke took a moment to listen to his surroundings. The only sounds he could hear were the crashing of the waves around the castle and the occasional squawk of a seagull. Once again, Luke lifted Max and carried him to the old wooden door which was barely hanging on by its hinges after taking a battering from the drones. Carefully poking his head out, Luke saw that the coast was clear.

Not wanting to take any chances, however, he made a dash for it, Max bobbing up and down as Luke ran across the courtyard. He couldn't help but notice the chips in the concrete at his feet, made by the drone's bullets.

They approached the hidden doorway, and Luke remembered this one didn't have a keypad. Using Max's hand as the key, he once again explored the wall and smiled when the doorway opened to let them through. Max had begun grunting and groaning, slowly waking up. Luke carried him into the castle and entered the first room he could find. It was a library. Hundreds of beautiful leather-bound books were in bookcases or fitted shelves that had been built into the walls. Two cosy red velvet armchairs were in front of an unlit fire. Luke placed Max into one and took the other for himself, enjoying the rest.

Max's eyes began to slowly open.

"Wh – where am I?" he asked.

"Disneyland. Don't you remember? You really wanted to go, so here we are."

Max looked around, confused.

"But, this is my library," he said. "I'm thirsty. Please, there's a small kitchen area through the door behind you."

Luke got up and opened the door. He found a fridge and took two bottles of water from it. He handed one to Max, who guzzled almost all of it in record time. Wiping his mouth, he gingerly began to move his body, wincing in discomfort.

"How did we get here?" he asked Luke.

"I carried you. What's the last thing you remember?"

Max thought for a moment, his face darkening.

"Felicity. It was Felicity."

"Well, at least I don't have to explain that to you. Yes, she betrayed us. You, Patrick, Carter and Aunt Sarah were then shot by that git Sebastian. He wanted me to think you were dead, but you were all shot with a tranquilizer dart. He then shot me. Only it didn't penetrate what appears to be my tough, dragon-like skin. Don't ask. I played dead whilst they loaded Patrick, Carter and Aunt Sarah into one truck with you and me in another. Felicity went with Sebastian in a car. Not too long after we left, I made my move. I beat up four Nazis, took some of their equipment, escaped the truck with you on my back, met a bloke called Eddie who drove us to the car park. I used your hands to get us through your security points and here we are. I thought we needed to get back to Patrick's Subcarine as quickly as we could."

Max stared at Luke in disbelief.

"You saved me?"

"It felt like the right thing to do. I'm sure you would've done the same for me."

"And you beat up four Nazis?"

"Yeah. It was awesome."

"I don't know what to say. Thank you."

"You're welcome. Perhaps you could start being nicer to me now? And to my aunt and Carter?"

Max smiled. "I'll try." He finished the rest of his water.

"I'm sorry about your wife," Luke said.

"My wife?"

Luke nodded as Max closed his eyes and rubbed his head.

"My wife. Of course, my wife!"

Max jumped up to his feet and promptly began wobbling. Luke got up to steady him.

"Luke, we need to go to my bedroom, immediately."

"Okay, that's weird. Why?"

"Felicity hasn't betrayed us. She's betrayed Sebastian!"

17

Max began walking towards the library's door. "Follow me and I'll explain on the way."

Max kept hold of Luke's arm as they left the library and walked into the hall. He wasn't particularly steady on his feet, but seemed to gather strength the further he walked.

"What's going on? What do you mean she hasn't betrayed us? I was there. I heard what she said and saw your face."

"You might have *heard* what she said, but you didn't *understand* what she said."

"Great, now you're sounding like Patrick."

"Felicity spoke about when we got engaged in Venice."

"So? I imagine a lot of people get engaged in Venice."

"You're right, only we've never been to Venice. We got engaged in New York."

"So why would she say Venice?"

"It was a message. Don't you see? Only I would know where we got engaged. Sebastian and the other Nazis certainly wouldn't. She was communicating in a way that only I would understand."

"Are you sure?"

"Of course I'm sure. I know where I got engaged, Luke. But that's not all," continued Max as they approached his bedroom. "She also told me to 'stay safe'. She never uses that expression. It's always, 'take care of yourself,' or something along those lines. We have a safe in our bedroom. I think she was telling me to look inside it."

Luke didn't look convinced, but kept his thoughts to himself. They entered the room, which was exactly as Luke had imagined. A huge four-poster bed occupied the middle of the space with solid oak chests and tables surrounding it. The bed was immaculately made and the heavy velvet curtains were open, allowing the sun to illuminate the entire room. Opposite the bed was a vanity desk with an assortment of grooming equipment. Above it was an oil painting of Max and Felicity, dressed as a king and queen from several hundred years ago.

"Wow." Luke saw it and didn't know what else to say. He turned his head so Max wouldn't see him laughing.

Max mistook Luke's derision for admiration.

"Wow, indeed. Isn't it magnificent?"

Luke steadied himself before answering.

"Yes. Yes, it is. And so subtle, too."

Max missed his sarcasm and began to bring the portrait down.

"Grab the other side, please," he said to Luke.

Together, they lowered the painting to the floor. Removing it revealed a safe that had been built into the brick wall. Max went to the combination and began twisting the dial into different positions until it clicked open.

"Seven-three-seven-nine?" Luke asked with a smile.

"How did you know that?"

"Lucky guess. But you might want to update your security codes in the future. Just a thought."

Max frowned at Luke and pulled out several documents from inside the safe. He went through them and was surprised to see an envelope with his name on it.

"Look," he said, holding it up to Luke.

"When was the last time you opened the safe?"

"I've no idea. Months and months ago. Perhaps even over a year."

"Well, it looks like Felicity has been in there much more recently. Open it. Remember, we still need to get out of here and rescue the others."

Max nodded and tore open the envelope. He began to read aloud.

"*My dearest Maxi. If you're reading this, then you've understood my clue and have escaped the Nazis. Things have probably happened that have made you confused and possibly even angry. First, you need to know that I absolutely and wholeheartedly love you and always have. Events seem to be happening quickly. Indeed, I believe Patrick is on his way here with Carter, Sarah and the Chosen One*," he looked up at Luke. "She wrote this only a few hours ago."

He continued reading the letter.

"*Sebastian will follow shortly after. I know this because I've spoken to him to tell him they're coming. This is all part of something much bigger than any of us, apart from maybe the Chosen One. This was Patrick's idea and I believe it to be the only way. I don't have time to explain everything now, but Patrick and I have been working together so I can get close to Sebastian. For the last few months, I have been feeding Sebastian information on the Guardians and the search for the Chosen One. Nothing too important, but enough to keep him interested. If the prophecy is to be believed, all of this will end soon, anyway. I couldn't tell you because your reaction needed to be genuine. I hope you can forgive me. Sebastian plans to sedate you and the others and take you to Berlin to find out what he can about the final challenge. The next total lunar eclipse is only two days away. That doesn't give you much time. I know you're capable enough to escape from the Nazis and hopefully, you rescued the Chosen One, too. It was my idea to make sure you were together in the truck. If you weren't, then all of this will probably be for nothing."*

"Awkward," smirked Luke.

"You must take him to the place where the quiet peas are. Say you have an appointment with Séamus (you can trust him) and take it from there. DO NOT COME TO GERMANY, IT'S TOO DANGEROUS.

Good luck and do your research.

All my love,

Felicity.

X."

"Max, I'm going to assume you know what Felicity's on about."

"I do. We have to go to London, immediately."

"Again? I've just come from there and it wasn't exactly a peaceful visit."

"This one will be. Well, it should be. Actually, it might not be."

"Brilliant."

"Let's gather some things and be on our way."

"Will we be using the Subcarine?"

"No. We'll take one of the Guardian's cars from the car park. We need to be quick, but not attract attention if we're to get where we need to go before it closes. The Subcarine will get us there quickly, but pulling out of the Thames with no one seeing us is highly unlikely."

Max began gathering a few bits and pieces and stuffing them into a bag. They then walked to the kitchen to gather some food and drinks for their journey.

"Right, Luke. Let's head back to the tunnel and I'll explain things on the way."

"If you say so. First things first, though. I need a wee."

"I should probably go too. This way."

The nearest bathroom wasn't far.

"After you," said Max, ushering Luke to the door.

"Okay, but can you not stand outside? I won't be able to go knowing you're there listening to me."

"Seriously?"

"Yes, seriously. Wait further away."

Max moved down the corridor, muttering under his breath. "Make sure you wipe the mess if you sprinkle!" he shouted to Luke.

"Yes, Aunt Sarah," Luke shouted back.

"Kids."

Luke finished his business, washed his hands, and left the bathroom. Max approached, looking suspicious.

"Don't worry, your Majesty. My aim was true."

Max looked doubtful, but went inside as Luke moved away. Max reappeared a few moments later, looking relieved in more ways than one.

"Shall we?" he asked Luke.

They made their way through the halls, into the courtyard, and finally into the church before descending into the tunnel once again.

"So, London. What's waiting for us there this time?" Luke asked.

"We're going to the London Library, and we're going to have to get a wiggle on if we're to get there before it closes."

"How do you know that's where we need to be?"

"Quiet peas."

"I only asked."

"What? No, because of the quiet peas. That's what Felicity wrote in her letter. It's another clue for me."

"Of course it is."

"The London Library is where the Guardians meet every now and then. There are numerous secret rooms there, many of which I've never been into. You'll think it's silly, but I made a joke there once that tickled Patrick so much, we thought he was having a heart attack."

"What was the joke?"

Max hesitated before speaking.

"What vegetables do librarians like?"

Luke stayed silent.

"Quiet peas." Max couldn't help but let out a chuckle when he said the punchline. It was met with silence by Luke.

"I can see why Patrick would've appreciated that," he finally responded.

"Indeed." Max was still giggling. "You know, there's nothing like a good joke."

"And that was nothing like a good joke."

"Felicity knew I'd remember that. She's a quite remarkable woman and infinitely braver than I realised."

Luke detected a choke in Max's voice. "We'll get her back, Max."

Max wheeled around and gripped Luke with a surprising intensity.

"Promise me you will, Luke. Promise me you'll do everything in your power to help her and stop Sebastian."

Luke was momentarily taken aback by seeing Max like this.

"I promise. But I'll need your help. I'm making this up as I go along and I can't do it alone."

Max nodded. "I'm here for you. Whatever you need."

The two shared a moment and continued down the tunnel.

"So, why the London Library? What's special about it?"

"Do you know anything about it at all?"

"Nope. Never heard of it. Should I?"

"Seriously, what do they teach you in school these days? If you spent more time off The Twitterbook, Tocky-Tick and Insta-YouTube, you might learn something."

"Wow. I think you might need to brush up on your social media knowledge."

"It's an independent library that was established in 1841. It also happens to be the largest lending library in Europe. Past members and presidents include William Makepeace Thackeray, T. S. Eliot, William Gladstone and even Charles Dickens. All Guardians."

"Charles Dickens was a Guardian?"

"He certainly was. And a very capable one too, by all accounts."

"That's pretty cool. Did you know his favourite drink was a martini?"

"How on earth do you know that?"

"I read about it in school. He walked into a bar and asked for one. The barman said, 'Olive or twist?'"

"Save it for Patrick. As I was saying, it's home to over one million books and acquires around 8,000 new items each year. They cover a plethora of subjects from fiction and architecture to topography and science. I'm assuming it's also the resting place of something that will help you and I understand what we're up against during the eclipse and that this Séamus will help us."

"Do you have any idea who he is?"

"I might."

"Well?"

"You'll see."

"Ugh, you're just like the others."

"In February 1944, the library was almost destroyed by a Nazi bomb. Not content with burning books, they wanted to blow them up as well."

"What do you mean?"

"In the 1930s, Nazi Germany and their Student Union conducted a campaign to burn books that opposed or contradicted the Nazi ideology. Thousands of works by dozens of Jewish authors as well as other nationalities and religions, including English and Irish writers, were thrown onto the pyre over the course of a few days."

"What is it with Nazis? They have some serious issues."

"You can say that again. Here we are."

They reached the end of the tunnel and made their way to the car park. Max moved towards a nondescript black saloon car. Using a remote control on a set of keys, he unlocked the doors, and the pair climbed in. After seeing Aunt Sarah's car and then Patrick's Subcarine, Luke was a little disappointed at how normal this one appeared.

"Does this car do anything other than drive?" he asked Max.

"I did say that we don't want to attract attention, but you needn't worry. She's got a few tricks up her sleeve if we need them. Right. If we have a good run, we'll be there in about five hours, give or take. I'm driving so I choose the music."

Max reached into the glove compartment and brought out a cd. Luke's heart sank when he saw it. It was Gilbert & Sullivan's *The Pirates of Penzance*. Luke had a feeling these next five hours were going to seem like five days.

18

Whilst Luke and Max were on their way to London, Sarah, Patrick and Carter had been driven for about an hour to Newquay airport and put on-board a private jet heading for Berlin. As they arrived in Newquay, the young Nazi officer that had opened the truck's doors only to find his unconscious comrades and two missing prisoners was momentarily lost for words. Gulping down his fear, he had approached Sebastian to tell him the news. Behind him, Felicity couldn't stop herself from smiling slightly at hearing the news.

Sebastian listened with unnerving calmness, keeping his eyes locked onto the young soldier.

"Thank you for informing me about this latest development. What is your name?"

"Obergefreiter Gruber."

"Please report to my office as soon as we arrive back at base, Obergefreiter Gruber."

The soldier's face turned pale.

"Yes, sir," he gave the Nazi salute and hurried away.

"So, Felicity," Sebastian turned to face her. "It would seem we have underestimated our enemy once again."

"It's a boy and my useless husband. We don't have any reason to panic."

"Perhaps. Perhaps not. The boy possesses certain skills and is proving himself quite capable. No matter. We have the old man and his aunt. We still have the advantage. Come. We shall be in Berlin in just a couple of hours where some friends of mine are awaiting our guests. They very much want to speak with them."

Felicity knew he meant Nazi doctors would be waiting to torture them for their knowledge. She shuddered. Her thoughts returned to her husband and Luke, finding comfort knowing they had outwitted Sebastian once again.

They boarded the jet, which had been painted red and black, to find the three prisoners still strapped to their gurneys. Sarah and Carter were stirring whilst Patrick remained unconscious. Sarah feebly lifted her head to take in her surroundings, surprised to find she hadn't been shot by a real bullet. Carter was doing the same. They looked at each other and briefly smiled.

"Luke? Where are you?" she called out.

"Your nephew is not here, Fräulein. I have other plans for him."

Sarah narrowed her eyes and stared at Sebastian. She let out a relieved laugh.

"He escaped, didn't he? Ha! Good for you, Luke. And he's got Max with him, too. Oh, you guys are in for it now."

"Hardly," replied Felicity. "With my worthless husband slowing him down they don't stand a chance."

"What happened to you, Felicity? Why are you doing this?" asked Sarah.

"I don't have to explain myself to the likes of you," she snapped.

"Max is a good man. Granted, he's an acquired taste, but he loves you. He didn't deserve this."

Inside, Felicity desperately wanted to go over to Sarah, to tell her everything was okay and that it was all an act, but she couldn't. Instead, she walked over to where she was lying and glared down at her.

"But you deserve everything that's coming and I can't wait to be there when they break you." she kept her eyes fixed on Sarah's but addressed Carter. "I hope you'll enjoy the show, Carter. You're going to watch her pain, her suffering. And then it will be your turn."

Carter struggled against his restraints, but they held firm. Felicity continued.

"How long do you think she'll last, hmm?"

When Carter spoke, his voice dripped with menace.

"Felicity. Your time will come. You don't know what you're up against, but you will."

"Oh, spare me, Carter," Felicity laughed. "You're a big boy, but you don't scare me."

"I wasn't talking about me. It's Luke you should be afraid of."

Felicity turned to look at him. "You all seem so sure of this boy, but that's all he is. A child."

"He's so much more than that, as you'll see."

The room descended into silence, which Sebastian broke.

"Well, I hope you all enjoy the short flight. I suggest you conserve your strength because, believe me, you are going to need it for what lies ahead."

He gave a malicious laugh and walked deeper into the plane with Felicity.

"Carter?" called Sarah.

"Yes?"

"I'm scared."

A different voice answered her. "You needn't be, my dear," Patrick said. "We'll come up with a plan to get out of here. Of that I'm sure."

"I'm scared for Luke, too," she added.

"Sarah, he's the Chosen One. We've already seen a glimpse of what he's capable of and he will continue to grow stronger each hour. That special young man is extraordinarily gifted. I'm extremely confident in his abilities and do not doubt that he will rise to the challenges in front of him."

19

"**I**'ve farted," confessed Luke.

"What? But, we're here. Couldn't you have held it in for a few more moments?"

"I've been holding it in for the past few hours! It was really hurting."

"For goodness' sake, Luke."

Max wound down the window and put his head outside, hoping the stench would escape quickly. It didn't.

"Sorry."

"Don't talk to me for a few moments. I don't want to open my mouth."

They had made the journey in just under six hours and both were a little stiff and irritable, especially Max, after Luke's toxic trump. Max found a pay-and-display parking space in St James's Square, close to the library. They walked in silence up some stone steps and through the double wooden doors, noting the opening hours on a sign. Luckily for them, the library was open until 9 pm.

They stood in the entrance hall, which led into the Reading Room, taking in the unique mix of old and new surrounding them. A maroon carpet supported numerous pillars that reached up to a high ceiling. In the middle of the room, and taking up most space, were large wooden desks with seats and individual lights for people to work at. Either side of the room, and reaching from the floor almost to the ceiling, were books. Hundreds, thousands of books. On each flank, metal staircases led to the first level where a thin wooden floor, barely wide enough to accommodate more than one person, ran along its length. Doors were leading to separate rooms, with another staircase opposite, rising to other floors.

A lady emerged from an office to their left. She was smiling and had the stereotypically conservative look of a librarian.

"Can I help you?" she asked them.

"Good evening. We have an appointment with Séamus," said Max.

"Of course. Please, sit down. I'll let him know you're here."

She went back into her office and picked up her phone.

Max and Luke sat on a leather sofa, which was just behind them, and waited. They didn't have to wait long. From one of the doors came an elderly man that was well over 6 feet tall and walked with the aid of an elaborately decorated cane. Limping towards them, Luke noticed that the head of the cane the man gripped in his left hand was carved into the shape of a dragon's head. He held out his other hand as he approached.

"Séamus Kelly. And you must be Max, which would make you Luke. It's an honour to meet you both."

Séamus had a slight Irish lilt in his voice, which reminded Luke of Patrick.

"How do you do?" asked Max.

"Hello," Luke said.

The three shook hands, Séamus wincing a little at the strength of Luke's grip.

"Ouch! Careful, Luke. My leg is ruined, let's not put my hand out of action too," he chuckled.

"Sorry."

"Well, let's find somewhere a bit more private, shall we? Walk this way. Well, perhaps without the limp, eh?" Séamus winked at Luke as he moved off towards the door he had emerged from. They walked along a series of corridors and down a flight of steps towards the library's basement.

"You need to be careful down here," laughed Séamus. "It's a labyrinth, is what it is. I've worked here all my life and I still get lost occasionally."

"It's magnificent," said Max.

"She's a wonderful place, that she is. Unless you don't like books, of course."

When they arrived at a metal door, Séamus typed an access code into the keypad and opened the door. It was a large room with portraits and photographs on two of the walls, whilst old books covered the other two. There was a long table in the centre with slots built into it, housing old newspapers and periodicals. Underneath the portraits was a desk with chairs and an easel to view large texts. Séamus closed the door behind them.

"I don't know how much you know about this place, but I assume you know she was bombed during the Second World War?"

"Yes, we knew that," answered Max.

"She took a lot of damage. Damn nearly finished her, but she's a sturdy one, that she is. February 23, 1944. A 500-pound bomb slammed into the library's central stack. We lost over 16,000 books that night, but I suppose it could've been a lot worse. Included in the loss were several biographies of people with names beginning with G to J as well as S to Z."

"G for George," whispered Luke.

"That's right," replied Séamus. "Fortunately, my father used to work here, and he was one of the first on the scene once the all-clear had been given. He was also a Guardian and knew exactly where he needed to go, hoping to find a book that had only recently been left in the library's possession and praying it hadn't been incinerated. Miraculously, in amongst the still smouldering ruins, he found the book perfectly preserved without a trace of any damage to it."

"That's impossible," said Luke.

"My boy, I think we live in a world where the impossible becomes possible nearly every day. I would have thought that you of all people would have realised that by now."

"What was the book? A biography of St George?" asked Max.

"Yes and no," Séamus cryptically replied.

"What do you mean?"

"Nobody can read it."

There was silence. Séamus laughed.

"Yes, I thought that might be your reaction, but it's true. It's most certainly a book. It has a cover and pages, but there's nothing written inside it. We've tried everything to get it to reveal its secrets, but nothing has worked."

"So how do you know it's a book about St George?"

"I'll show you."

Séamus turned his back on them and walked towards a photograph of a distinguished-looking gentleman with a silver beard and hair.

"This is Thomas Carlyle, the main founder of the London Library." He removed the frame to reveal a safe behind it. As he entered the code, he continued talking. "Prior to this place, Carlyle would use the library at the British Museum. He didn't like it much. Too cramped, not enough seats, the catalogues were a disorganised mess, and you weren't allowed to borrow any books! What sort of library doesn't let you borrow books? Anyway, together with a few influential friends, they established the London Library, and she's been thriving ever since."

The safe contained just one book, which he carefully brought out. He handed it to Max as Luke joined him to examine it.

It was the size of a regular paperback novel, but much thinner. Luke estimated that it only contained about 50 pages. Its cover was like leather and was also slightly rough, as if it were pitted with tiny dots. On the front was the unmistakable image of a dragon. Although it was quite faded, it was an exquisite drawing and almost looked life-like. The dragon's worn yellow eyes stared dully back at Max and Luke. On the back cover was the equally recognisable flag of St George, its red cross nothing but a dull and faded memory of what once was. Max opened the book and scanned the contents.

"You're right. There's absolutely nothing written on these pages."

"Can I see?" asked Luke.

Max handed the book to Luke and went to speak with Séamus. Luke held the book and felt a warmth coming from it. The dragon's yellow eyes began to shine with an unnerving intensity, as if it were looking into Luke's very soul. Turning the book over, the flag now shone a majestic shade of red, glorious in its brilliance. Luke slowly opened the book and was stunned to see the pages filled with words and illustrations.

"Woah," he breathed.

"Everything alright, Luke?" Max asked.

Before he could answer, the door opened and in walked the lady that had spoken to Max and Luke earlier when they arrived.

"Séamus, thank goodness I've found you," she said, her voice trembling slightly.

She was clearly frightened about something.

"What is it, Pamela?"

"Remember, you asked me to keep a lookout for groups of men acting suspiciously?"

Séamus nodded.

"Well, there are three men upstairs now asking for you. I tried to tell them you weren't working today, but they didn't believe me and one of them started to get quite angry and insisted I bring you to them. I pretended the phone wasn't working, so I had to go and find you."

"And what did they look like?"

"They looked very strong and intimidating. They were wearing black suits with strikingly red shirts and black ties and I'm sure I heard them conversing in what sounded like German."

Luke and Max shared a look.

"We need to leave, now," said Max.

"Well done, Pamela. I just need you to do one more thing for me," said Séamus.

"Anything, Séamus."

The way she said that made Luke think there was more than a professional relationship between these two.

"Please take our two guests here to vault 713 and show them the exit."

"Of course. Follow me, you two."

"Will you be alright?" asked Luke.

"'Course I will. Those Nazi goons might've given me this limp, but I gave them an awful lot worse. Best of luck with the book."

"Thanks for your help, Séamus," Max said. "We're grateful."

They shook hands and left the room. Just as they were about to go their separate ways, Séamus called after them.

"Luke. When you see my brother, tell him I forgive him and that we'll have a drink soon."

"Your brother?" Luke was puzzled.

"Perhaps some of his Bushmills," he said with a smile.

Luke suddenly realised who Séamus was referring to.

"Your brother's Patrick?"

"That he is. Go on, now. I'll buy you some time with this lot."

They waved goodbye to each other.

"Come on, you two. Vault 713 is this way," Pamela said as she moved off deeper into the library.

"Did you know he was Patrick's brother?" Luke asked Max.

"Of course. Wasn't that obvious?"

"Not to me."

"Crikey, Luke. Keep up. So, Pamela. What exactly is in vault 713?" Max asked.

"It houses a small amount of incredibly rare and ancient manuscripts dating back to before Jesus Christ, but it's also an escape route that only senior members of staff know about. You two must be very important or in lots of danger for Séamus to do this."

"Do you mean to say you're not a –"

Before Luke could say, "Guardian," Max interrupted him.

"That you're not sure who we are?"

"No. I'm just helping Séamus. He's been very kind to me since I started working here. I don't like to pry and it really isn't any of my business."

There was a pause, and then Pamela spoke again.

"Why? Who are you?"

"I think it's best Séamus explains," answered Max diplomatically.

"Perhaps you're right."

They continued in silence until they reached a nondescript door that looked more like the entrance to the cleaning cupboard than a room holding centuries-old treasures. Pamela typed in some numbers on the keypad and opened the door. The inside was as unimpressive as the door. All four walls and the ceiling were painted black, and the only light came from a dim LED bulb that had activated as the door opened. The only item in the room was a safe as big as a chest of drawers in the centre of the floor. Pamela walked past it towards the far wall. She began running her hands along the wall as if she were looking for something.

"What are you doing?" Luke asked.

"I'm looking for the lock to the secret door. Ah, here it is."

Pamela pulled on the hidden latch and a door swung outwards, revealing some stone steps leading downwards. A waft of cold air blew out to greet them.

"Be careful going down the steps. There are about eight of them and if you fall, you'll know about it. Follow the path for about ten minutes and you'll come to another set of steps like these. Look for the hidden latch and the door will open into some disused toilets in Green Park near the tube station. There are motion-activated LED lights in the tunnel to guide your way."

At this, Luke gave Max an 'I told you so' look and smirked.

"Well, it was jolly nice to meet you both, whoever you are. Any friend of Séamus is a friend of mine. I'll close the door behind you."

"Thank you, Pamela," said Max.

"Thanks, Pamela. Bye!" Luke said.

They went through the door, into the tunnel, using the light to walk down the steps. Pamela closed the door and began her journey back to the library.

Walking back through the basement's corridors, Pamela's thoughts turned to the three men she had spoken to upstairs in the library. Who were they and what did they want with Séamus? They didn't seem like the type of people you should cross, so she hoped he wasn't in any kind of trouble. He had always been so kind to her. They enjoyed each other's company and she was sure there was a certain spark between them. Both had lost their previous partners and were in their twilight years. Pamela was lonely and thought Séamus must be too. She'd recently been thinking about asking him to dinner. But those men. She shivered as she recalled how they had spoken to her. Fearful for Séamus, she quickened her pace as all sorts of awful images filled her head.

As she opened the door to the library, Pamela instantly sensed that something was wrong. The usual silence that greeted her ears was still there, but this time there was a menacing air included. And the library users had gone. All of them. It wasn't until she walked further into the Reading Room she saw why the atmosphere was so strange. Down at the far end and away from the windows, Séamus was tied to a chair and was bleeding from a cut above his left eye. Two men were standing in front of him, one holding a gun pointed at Séamus. Pamela was just about to scream when a hand clamped tightly around her mouth. It was the third man who had been waiting for her to come back. The man had a gun prodding painfully into her ribs as he marched her towards the others. Séamus wearily raised his head as she approached.

"Ah, Pamela. I'm so pleased to see you again. Please, take a seat and get comfortable. I'd be grateful if you wouldn't scream because not only will that hurt my ears, you will also anger my friend here and it's in your best interests for that not to happen," said the one man who wasn't holding a gun.

A terrified Pamela was lowered into a chair opposite Séamus and tied up.

"My name is Erich and I would like you to tell me why the man and the boy were here and where they have gone. If you don't, I will hurt you. So, why were they here and where have they gone?" he smiled pleasantly enough, but he oozed menace.

Pamela's mouth was open, but no sound was coming out. She began to sob.

"Pamela, it will be alright," soothed Séamus.

"No, Pamela. It will not be alright," said Erich. "I am not a patient man. Please answer my question."

"I – I – I don't know why they were here," Pamela answered.

Erich looked at her with false pity.

"Shoot her in the knee," he ordered.

"No!" screamed Séamus. "I'll tell you everything. Just leave her alone, please."

Séamus quickly began telling Erich about the empty book and their escape via vault 713. Erich listened intently. He nodded to one of his colleagues who clubbed Pamela on the head with the butt of his gun, knocking her out.

"Pamela!" Séamus wailed.

"Untie him."

The other man did so and Séamus immediately checked on Pamela to see if she was alright. Her pulse was strong. She would be fine.

"What sort of man attacks an elderly woman?" Séamus looked at Erich with pure hatred.

"I take no pleasure in doing so. This is merely business. Now. You will lead us to vault 713, immediately or poor Pamela will be shot and it will be because of you."

Séamus tenderly stroked Pamela's face and made a silent promise to himself that if he came through this, he would finally pluck up the courage to ask her to dinner.

"It's this way," Séamus said as he moved off towards the door that would take them to the basement. They made their way through the corridors until they reached the vault. Séamus unlocked the hidden door and begrudgingly told them where the passage came out.

"Thank you, Séamus. You have been most helpful."

Séamus sensed the blow just before it came, but could do nothing about it. He too was cracked on the head and knocked unconscious. As he slumped to the floor, the three men descended the steps into the tunnel. Guns at the ready, they moved as quickly as they could in pursuit of Luke and Max.

20

Sarah, Carter and Patrick had arrived in Berlin and were being transported to a secret Nazi headquarters. They were taken to a huge and foreboding castle in a forest, found to the west of the city, untied and marched into the building at gunpoint. Aunt Sarah and Carter were desperately looking for escape opportunities, but had to admit that things were looking bleak for them. Patrick was admiring the many tapestries that were hanging from the stone walls, most of them showing a stern-looking Adolf Hitler.

"How remarkable. To think the Führer himself once walked these very steps," he observed.

"This was one of my great-grandfather's favourite retreats," Sebastian said as he emerged from a doorway in front of them, with Felicity and several soldiers behind him.

"That's ironic," Sarah began. "Because that's what he and his lunatic bunch of fanatics did when the war was lost, wasn't it? Retreat."

Felicity barged past Sebastian, a look of fury written on her face.

"Stop, Felicity," ordered Sebastian. "I do not want my guest to get hurt before she gets hurt. If you would all be so kind as to follow me. You have an appointment with a doctor."

Sebastian and Felicity led the way towards a large wooden door. Sebastian opened it, and they all moved inside. Three chairs were waiting for them, positioned in a triangle formation so they could all see each other. Sarah, Carter and Patrick were each placed in a chair and secured to it. From another door, a man wearing a white overall entered, wheeling in a trolley with a frightening array of surgical equipment on it. He moved into the centre of the three prisoners. As he began to prepare a syringe with a clear liquid in it, Sebastian spoke.

"My friends, this is Doctor Karl Mengele. Perhaps you are familiar with his grandfather, Josef?"

A stunned silence greeted these words as Aunt Sarah, Carter, and Patrick shared a moment. Josef Mengele was an SS officer and physician during the Second World War. He was primarily stationed at Auschwitz concentration camp, where he became known as the Angel of Death because of his abhorrent and evil actions towards those kept captive. After Germany's defeat, Mengele fled to South America where he somehow lived for 30 years until his death in 1979.

"Yes, I thought that might get your attention," Sebastian continued. "Soon, you will all be telling me everything you know about the prophecy. I shall leave you in the capable hands of the good doctor for the time being and will return soon. Felicity, come."

Felicity stared deep into Sarah's eyes.

"Felicity, please," whispered Sarah.

Felicity moved towards Sarah.

"Doctor Mengele? Start with this one first," she said.

With one final smirk, Felicity left, closing the door behind her. Sarah, Carter, and Patrick were now left alone with Doctor Mengele and his instruments of terror.

21

"It can't be much further, can it?" Luke asked.

"I wouldn't have thought so. We've been walking for almost 10 minutes so, according to Pamela, we should see the steps soon."

"What will we do next?"

"Well, I imagine we need to find some transport, get to somewhere safe and examine that book to see if we can uncover its secrets."

"Oh, I can read it alright," said Luke.

"What? You can? Why didn't you tell me before? We've been walking for ages."

"You didn't ask."

"We really need to work on our communication."

"I haven't looked properly, but when I touched the book it sort of came to life."

"Go on," Max urged.

"Well, the colours on the front and back covers became bright, and I only had a quick look inside, but I saw some writing and illustrations. One drawing looked like it was a full moon."

"They weren't kidding when they said you were full of surprises."

"Do you know where to go when we get out of here?"

"I do. There's a –" Max stopped talking as he saw Luke had spun around. "What is it?"

"Quiet," Luke hissed.

He squinted and with his newly improved vision saw the LED lights from way behind them, quickly switching back on in sequence.

"What are you looking at? There's nothing but darkness back there," said Max.

"Not anymore. We're being followed. And by someone in a hurry. We need to move, fast."

They turned and began to move as quickly as they could through the passageway. Bullets slammed into the walls and floor behind them. The men chasing them were shooting, but were still too far away for their bullets to be effective. But it wouldn't take long until they would be. They reached the steps and, after they ran up them, Max searched for the hidden lock. They could now hear running footsteps getting closer, and the lights were visible to Max as well.

"I don't want to hurry you, but you need to get this door open or we're in big trouble."

"What do you think I'm doing? I'm looking."

"Well, look better!"

Finally, Max's fingers found the latch, and the hidden door swung open to reveal the most disgusting public toilets Luke had ever seen. Luke slammed the door shut behind him.

"That stench is disgusting," he exclaimed.

"It's almost as bad as what you did in the car, Luke."

"I thought these were disused? Smells like they're constantly being used and perhaps someone's even using them right now. I reckon it's the devil. Only he could make that smell. Or my friend Charlie."

They exited the toilets into Green Park, not too far from Buckingham Palace, and gratefully sucked in the fresh air.

"We need to get on to the streets as quickly as possible to lose them," said Max. "This way."

They made their way out of the park onto the ever-busy Piccadilly.

"There are far too many people around here. Even the Nazis aren't stupid enough to start a gunfight in the heart of London at this time of day," stated Max. "We'll head to Green Park tube station. There's a secret entrance –"

"Another one?" interrupted Luke.

"Another one. There's a secret entrance near the platforms that will lead us to an abandoned station called Down Street. It was closed in 1932, although Winston Churchill used it during the war and referred to it as 'The Barn.' The Guardians have been using it as a safe house ever since. It will also have some much-needed supplies. We need to go there and regroup."

"And then rescue the others."

"I fear there may not be time for that, Luke. Let's just take one thing at a time, okay? Here, you'll need this to get through the barriers."

They entered the station, and Max handed Luke what looked like a debit card. It was the same size and weight, but rather than numbers, a chip and a magnetic stripe, it just had a very faint outline of a dragon on it. Luke gave a wry smile and noted that being a Guardian meant free travel on London's travel network. Bonus. As they touched their cards onto the pads and the gates swung open for them, they had no idea that the three men pursuing them had just glimpsed them walking into the station. They discreetly followed Max and Luke at a distance, preparing to confront them before they boarded a train.

22

Doctor Mengele was hunched over his instruments, filling three syringes with a clear liquid. He had ignored all attempts by Sarah and Carter to engage him in conversation, his silence somehow making the situation even more sinister. Patrick appeared deep in thought, concentration etched on his face.

"Patrick? I don't know what you're doing over there, but if you have any bright ideas, then now would be the time to share them," Carter said.

"Things could be worse," Patrick responded.

"Worse? How could they possibly be worse than this?"

"Well, they could have split us up. At least this way we're all here and can spend some quality time together."

Patrick's eyes glinted mischievously. It was then Sarah and Carter knew their situation was hopeless. They were in very serious trouble indeed, so they did the only thing they could think of. They began to laugh. All three of them. It started as a small giggle and gradually built up into hysterics, the trio with tears streaming down their faces. Doctor Mengele watched them with an empty detachment, a full syringe in his hand. He let their laughter die before addressing them. His voice was deceptively soothing.

"This will not be pleasant for any of you. I am about to inject you with a complex mixture of Sodium Pentothal and other, shall we say, legally questionable compounds. Some you may know; others are of my creation."

"It's a truth serum," stated Carter.

"Yes. An extremely potent serum. Soon you will tell us everything you know about the prophecy and the upcoming eclipse. There are, unfortunately for you, some rather unpleasant side effects. During observations on our test subjects, they all exhibited the same behaviour once the serum had worn off."

He paused, allowing the tension to rise. Nobody spoke.

"Don't ask it, Carter," urged Patrick.

"I need to know. He can't leave it like that. What were the side effects?"

"I'm so pleased you asked. Every one of our patients, sadly, lost their minds."

Patrick shot Carter a look. "Happy now? I would much rather have gone through this not knowing what was going to happen to me."

Carter once again began to strain against his bonds, but he was firmly held in place.

"Now, I believe I am to start with you, Fräulein. Once injected, the serum will soon work its way into your system and when Sebastian returns, you will tell us everything we need to know. Not long after that, the pain will start and you will be locked in a permanent state of insanity for the rest of your days. You will have just enough of your old self left to realise something isn't quite right, but not enough to do anything about it. I do not envy you."

He began to advance on Sarah, who was panicking, her

breaths coming quickly and sharply. Carter was screaming her name whilst Patrick looked helplessly on. Suddenly, there was what sounded like a muted gunshot, and Doctor Mengele stopped moving, a quizzical expression on his face. His knees buckled, and he crumpled to the floor soundlessly. Sarah, Carter and Patrick looked around them in confusion when from a doorway in a darkened corner of the room emerged a figure wearing a German army uniform and holding a silenced pistol. It was Obergefreiter Gruber, the soldier due to report to Sebastian. He looked scared and his hands were shaking.

"Thank you, young man," Patrick spoke quietly so as not to startle him. "I'm Patrick. What's your name?"

"Gruber. Serge Gruber."

"A splendid name. Serge, would you be so kind as to help us out of these bindings? They're rather uncomfortable."

Serge cautiously made his way around Doctor Mengele's body, making sure he didn't look at it.

"Would you also mind holstering your pistol, Serge? Guns have a nasty habit of going off around us at the moment."

Serge did and then produced a knife from his belt. He cut the bonds holding Patrick, Sarah, and then Carter. Carter immediately disarmed Serge and quickly put him into a chokehold.

"Why are you doing this?" he asked Serge.

Carter's enormous arm was wrapped around Serge's neck, making it hard for him to speak.

"Sebastian was going to kill me. I was in charge when your friends escaped, so he held me responsible. If you're asked to go to his office after something goes wrong, you're never heard from again," he spluttered.

"Why should we believe you?"

"Why would I lie? I've just killed Doctor Mengele. Doesn't that tell you something?"

"Carter, let the young man breathe," said Patrick.

Carter reluctantly eased his grip on Serge as Sarah relieved him of his pistol and pointed it at him. Serge rubbed his neck.

"You must know that not all of us here share Sebastian's ideologies. I never wanted to be a soldier, but I was left with no choice. I'll explain more later, but we need to leave this place before Sebastian returns."

"I don't like this," growled Carter.

"We have no choice. Staying here is not an option anymore," answered Patrick.

"Fine. But know that I'll be watching your every move. If you trick us, you die."

"I understand. Follow me."

He moved back into the corner towards the door he had appeared from. Patrick stopped briefly to look at Doctor Mengele's body and picked up the syringe he had been carrying. Emptying it on the floor, he went to the doctor's table of instruments and poured away the rest of the truth serum.

23

Luke and Max walked down the escalator, heading for the westbound Piccadilly line platform. The station was busy with its usual mix of commuters and tourists. They kept their voices low as Max discussed their next move.

"We need to be careful and quick, but more importantly, discreet. At the end of the platform is a door built into the wall. Like you've already seen, it's opened by placing a hand in the correct place. It will open and close quickly, so don't hang about. There's a train arriving in a few minutes. We'll time our moment when it's busiest as people are leaving and boarding the train. It will then be a cramped but quick walk to Down Street station. Questions?"

"Won't we be seen on CCTV?"

"No. We've taken care of that. Once the palm print is read, an electronic burst will scramble their security system for the time it will take us to get behind the door."

"Seems like it's not just me that's full of surprises."

They made their way onto the platform, where the indicator told them they had two minutes to wait, and got into position. As they waited, Luke sensed danger.

"Max. Something's about to happen."

Just then, Erich and his two colleagues entered the platform and headed towards them.

As they approached, Luke whispered to Max. "Follow my lead and be ready to open the door."

"Good evening, gentlemen. I am here for the book you have in your possession. If you do not offer it freely, I shall use force. You will also give me your tooth."

"You can't handle the tooth," Max quipped.

"You what?" Luke whispered, and looked at Max.

"It's a pun. A famous quote from a Tom Cruise film. It's actually a very clever joke."

"It's only clever if you get it."

There was one minute left before the next train arrived.

"Yes, I was warned to expect English humour. I'm pleased you've lived up to my rather low expectations."

"What is it with you lot? Don't you find anything funny?"

"You won't be laughing, Luke, when you're bleeding out on this filthy platform and I have your book and the tooth."

Max was readying himself for something he knew was coming. He could hear the rumble of the approaching train. Luke pulled the book from one of his pockets and held it in front of him. The train was even closer now and Luke had to shout to make himself heard.

"If you want it, go and get it!"

As the train noisily pulled into the platform, Luke threw the book as far as he could over the heads of Erich and the other two. As all three watched it sail over them, the train stopped and opened its doors. Dozens of people poured out, some barging their way through the crowds, whilst others expertly manoeuvred their way around the human obstacle course. The book landed about 20 metres behind Erich and the three men frantically went after it as the book was unknowingly kicked about, edging dangerously close to the platform's edge. As the train doors began to close and it prepared to move off, Erich dived to reach the book just as it was about to fall onto the track. He caught it as it fell, relief washing over him. Clutching his prize and showing it to his colleagues, his joy turned to frustration when he saw that Luke and Max had vanished.

As soon as Luke had thrown the book, Max quickly opened the door and the two of them had scrambled through it and into a small, dark and ancient passageway.

"Why did you do that? Now they have the book!" Max was furious.

"No, they haven't. They have *a* book, not *the* book. Look." Luke pulled out the real book from another pocket.

"What? When? How? Why?"

"Um, let me answer that in order. I threw a different book because I picked up a decoy back at the library because I thought it might come in useful. Turns out I was right."

"I really must stop underestimating you."

They carried on walking, using torches Max had brought with them to light their way. After a few minutes, they reached the end and Max unlocked another door that opened into what was once an office. Although it was a small room, there was still enough space for a table and several chairs around it. They could hear the rumble of trains passing by from only a few feet away. Max switched on a light from a switch on the wall. The bare bulb hanging from the ceiling burst into life. They both took a seat.

"Quite amazing to think that Winston Churchill himself sat at this table, don't you think?"

"I suppose so."

"Well, don't get too carried away, will you?"

"I'm thinking about the others."

"Of course. Sorry. So, the book?"

Luke held it up, showing Max the now glowing colours on both the front and back covers. As he handed it over, the colours instantly faded. Luke took the book back and the magnificent features came to life again.

"Amazing," said Max.

Max got up and moved to sit next to Luke, producing two bottles of water from his bag. Luke opened the book and began to look through it. It began with several drawings of dragons, all finished with exquisite detail by somebody who was an incredibly talented artist. The dragons were of different sizes and colours, but all had a vicious look about them that showcased their menace. The last drawing before some text began was an interpretation of St George killing the dragon, his arm inside the beast's mouth with his lance having pierced its neck. Its mouth was clamped around George's arm, whose face was screwed up in agony, blood dripping from his wound. Luke began to read the writing.

"*I, Florentia, wife of George and mother of Angelus and Victor, have little time left in this world. My dearest husband is now at peace, free of the visions that have haunted his dreams, and I shall be by his side soon, God willing. My tale shall be brief, for I lack the strength to speak for long. I can only hope that what I say will aid the Chosen One when the time comes. My dearest son Angelus is here with me, scribing my words. Our bloodline and legacy shall continue thanks to the grandchildren I have been blessed with, but it would seem our family has a rift that will never heal.*

"*Our eldest son, Angelus, is a loving and kind man, bound to protect the dragon's tooth which he now wears around his neck, with his life. The very tooth that my husband recently passed unto him.*

"His younger brother, Victor, has grown into a cruel and evil man, corrupted by the power of his blood and his quest to possess the tooth.

"When he tried and failed to take the tooth through force, he and his family were banished by his father, the heartache of him doing so contributing to his failing health and passing. Where they are now we do not know, although there are whispers they are in Germania. I must tell whoever is reading this that Victor can never possess the tooth. He is too dangerous and not to be trusted.

Before he passed, George and I agreed the tooth shall be hidden and its hiding place kept secret, save for those that need to know. For one day, the prophecy will be fulfilled and the Chosen One must possess the tooth to prevent eternal darkness.

I must now inform you that there is one piece of information that has been hidden from all, even Angelus. The dragon that was slain by my fearless husband gave another tooth. As the dragon's body was being cremated, George and I noticed that two teeth were missing. Where this second is, alas, we do not know. We returned to the battleground and searched, but found it not. This one may not possess the same powers as ours, but we must assume it does. This tooth must be found and kept as safe as possible. Certainly, it must remain out of the grasp of those with evil intentions. We must be grateful Victor did not know about this.

The Prophecy shall be passed from Guardian to Guardian, but Angelus will share it here when I have finished my words.

My husband's final dream before his passing spoke of the ancient stones from his first vision and of green fields. I have drawn what I heard below. I know not of this place, but perhaps when the time comes, the Chosen One will be familiar with this area.

With this information about the stones, George also spoke. His words were thus: 'With the tooth and the blood a choice must be made, if the wrong one is taken, all hope will fade. Choose wisely and all shall be right, darkness will lift, in its place, light.'

To whoever is reading this; find the missing tooth before it's too late and, for the sake of all you hold dear, make the right choice. I'm sorry I don't have more for you.

May God be with you,

Florentia"

The original prophecy that Aunt Sarah had recited for Luke followed and Luke and Max both let out a deep breath after reading Florentia's words. They sat in silence for a while.

"Well, at least we know where this ritual or challenge needs to take place," said Max. "Stonehenge. That drawing couldn't be any clearer. But this missing tooth is going to be a problem."

"Is there Wi-Fi here?"

"Of course."

Luke pulled out his phone, found the network, and asked for the password.

"3-0-1-1-1-8-7-4. Churchill's birthday. Yes, this new tooth is going to require all our cunning and guile if we are to work out where to find it. Although it'll be like searching for a needle in a haystack. It could be anywhere by now. Literally, anywhere. Sydney, Cairo, New York or Rio de Janeiro. How the hell are we supposed to figure out where, exactly?" Max was becoming increasingly agitated. "Perhaps there's more information in the book? We need to go through it again. Maybe Patrick has information we could use. Talk about mission impossible. The eclipse is only about 24 hours away. What chance do we have? Damn it!"

"Found it," Luke said.

He had logged on to the internet and begun a search of museums and teeth of unknown origins. After scrolling through several pages, something caught his eye, and he felt the warmth of his tooth against his skin.

"Oh. That was easy. Are you sure?"

"Positive. Finding it *was* easy, but getting it is another matter. You're not going to believe this. We have to break into the Natural History Museum."

24

S erge walked with urgency along several stone corridors, with Carter behind him, followed by Patrick and Sarah. Carter had taken the pistol and kept it aimed at Serge the whole time. Sarah was lost in her thoughts, dwelling on Felicity's betrayal. Patrick noticed and seemed to read her mind.

"Sarah, there's something you need to know about Felicity."

"What's the evil witch done now?"

"It's my pleasure to inform you that your friend Felicity is still your friend Felicity."

"What are you talking about?"

"She has not betrayed us. In fact, Felicity has been working undercover for the Guardians and spying on Sebastian at my request for several months now."

A stunned silence followed this bombshell.

"She's what?" asked Carter.

"I conceived the idea a long time ago and Felicity jumped at the chance to be involved with some fieldwork for a change. After all, who would suspect poor, meek

Felicity as being a master of deception? I secretly trained her in preparation for her mission and I'm delighted to say that she has excelled in her role. Why, she even managed to fool her own husband."

"I don't know what to say. That's incredibly brave of her."

"Indeed, Sarah. We must hope she successfully comes through this unscathed."

"We need to help her. Now."

"Alas, Felicity is on her own. She knows this. If we attempt to rescue her now, we may place her in further danger. This needs to play out naturally."

"That doesn't seem right or fair."

"I know, my dear, but that is how it must be. Now, then. What exactly is your plan, Serge?"

"I'm working on it."

"Ah. Well, do you think you might be able to rustle up some more weapons and perhaps a satellite phone?"

"We'll have to go to the armoury. If we hurry, that should be possible."

"Splendid."

They walked until they reached a large door built into the wall. Serge turned to face them. "I know this will be hard, but you're going to have to trust me. We can't go out there like this. You need to give me my gun and keep your hands behind your back."

Carter glared at Serge, but at a nod from Patrick, reluctantly handed him his pistol.

"Thank you. Beyond this door is the armoury where you can choose some weapons and your satellite telephone. It will be manned, but leave that to me."

He opened the door and ushered the group out ahead of him. They were in a courtyard that had smaller buildings attached to the main one they had just left.

"Head to the building ahead of you on the right," Serge instructed.

Sarah, Carter and Patrick did so. Occasionally, pairs of soldiers passed them by and greeted Serge. At one point, one of his superior officers stopped him to ask where he was heading. Serge told him he was following Sebastian's orders to transfer them to a more secure location, which he accepted and moved on.

They stopped outside of the armoury, and Serge knocked on the door. A young soldier, similar in age to Serge, but slightly older and still carrying some puppy fat, opened it. He greeted Serge with a warm smile.

"Serge, my friend. How nice to see you. How can I help you on this fine evening?"

"Guten Abend, Michael. I'm afraid this isn't a social call."

Michael looked puzzled and then shocked as Serge raised his gun and pointed it at his friend's face. He hurried into the room, followed by the others.

"Serge? What are you doing?"

"I'm truly sorry. I really am. Sebastian was going to have me executed in the morning for my failure in a mission."

"Well, I don't think he's going to be shaking your hand when he finds out what you've done here," answered Michael.

"Bravo! I like this one," laughed Patrick.

"We're going to take some weapons, a satellite phone and we need the keys to the Beast."

"You'll never get away with this, Serge. Please reconsider," urged Michael.

"It's too late. I can't stay here. With them, I have a chance. Come with us, Michael."

"Woah, there. This is going to be hard enough with the four of us. Five is virtually impossible," said Carter.

"My place is here. Take what you need, but please do not kill me," begged Michael.

"Kill you? Of course not. But I'm afraid we can't allow you to raise the alarm just yet. Tell me, is the Beast ready to go?"

"Of course. I saw to her myself earlier today."

"Thank you."

Carter and Sarah took some weapons whilst Patrick found a fully charged satellite phone.

"Michael, again, I'm truly sorry about this. Perhaps when all this is over, we shall see each other again."

"Make it quick –"

But before he could finish, Carter clobbered him on the head with the butt of his gun, knocking him out.

"Forgive me, Michael," Serge whispered.

"Thank you, Serge," said Patrick. "Now, about this Beast?"

"It's an armoured vehicle capable of great speed. We only have one here, so I think it will be perfect to make our escape. The garages are not far, but we must hurry. Sebastian will soon realise you are missing."

Sarah and Carter did their best to conceal their weapons whilst Patrick examined the satellite phone. As they left, Serge picked up some guns and took one last look at his friend, motionless on the floor.

"Goodbye, Michael."

Walking back out into the courtyard, Patrick tried to hide his slight frame in between Carter and Sarah as he quickly typed some numbers into the phone and raised it to his ear.

25

"W e have to what?"

"We have to break into the Natural History Museum. That's where the tooth is. Look."

Luke showed Max his phone with an image of the ancient tooth stating that it was kept at London's famous museum.

"How can you be sure?"

"A feeling." Luke reached up to touch the tooth around his neck.

"If you're sure, then I trust you. We just need to figure out how to do this."

"Do you have any contacts that work there? Surely it would make sense to have Guardians placed at museums around the world in case of new discoveries or significant findings."

"You're absolutely right, and we do. But at this time of night, they won't be working and the museum is already closed. We can't wait until the morning for this."

As Luke placed the book on the table, he noticed a small

gap in between two of the pages. Opening it, a tiny scrap of parchment fell to the ground. The paper was ancient and blank. Luke picked it up and once again words began to form as if woken by his touch. He began reading. *"Victor knows about the second tooth. He took my children. I had no choice but to tell him of its existence. Be aware that he and his descendants will not stop in their quest to find it. I'm Sorry. Angelus."*

"Well that complicates things," Max said.

"Does it? They obviously haven't found it because if they had we'd know about it, right?"

"Right."

"And we're the only ones that know where it is, right?"

"Right."

"So, there's no problem. We just keep it to ourselves, right?"

"Yes, I suppose you're right, Luke," agreed Max.

In another room, a telephone rang. The pair looked at each other in surprise. They walked along some narrow corridors, following the sound. It led them to the old Telephone Exchange room which was covered in decades of grime. In amongst the time-worn wires were several, very much out of place, satellite phones in charging docks. It was one of those that was ringing now. Max tentatively reached out a hand and picked up the handset.

"Hello?"

His eyes widened, and a broad smile lit up his face. It was Patrick.

"Patrick! Where are you?"

"Germany. We don't have much time, Max. Is Luke safe?"

"Yes, he's with me. He saved my life. How did you know we'd be here?"

"Bravo, young Luke. I dialled the fail-safe emergency number.

There are several in secret places hidden around the world. I thought it was worth a shot. I'm assuming you've found Churchill's Barn?"

"Yes, we're in Down Street Station. Felicity hasn't betrayed us. She's still a Guardian and is working against Sebastian."

"Yes, dear boy, I know. It was my idea, remember?"

"Oh, yes. Sorry. We saw your brother and have the book. Three of Sebastian's goons tried to stop us, but we escaped. Again, thanks to Luke."

"Have you been able to read it?"

"Yes. We need to go to Stonehenge for the eclipse, but we don't know what will happen when we get there apart from that Luke will need to make some sort of choice. But there's something you need to know. There's another tooth at the Natural History Museum. We need to get it before Sebastian finds out about it so we're heading there now."

"Another tooth? Goodness, that's unexpected. Sarah, Carter and our new friend Serge will meet you at Stonehenge if we get out of here. We have approximately 24 hours."

"What about Felicity?"

"Don't worry about her, Max. She's more resourceful than you realise."

"She sure is."

"Good luck and we'll see you soon."

Patrick ended the call.

"So much for keeping the new tooth and its whereabouts to ourselves," Luke raised his eyebrows at Max.

"It was Patrick. I think we can trust him. Anyway, they're all fine and have even made a friend called Serge. They're in Germany and heading for Stonehenge."

Luke breathed a sigh of relief.

"And Felicity?"

"She's on her own, but I have every confidence in her."

"So do I, Max. She'll be fine."

Max nodded his thanks. "Let's find a supply room and stock up. There's bound to be one or two items that can help us during the next stage."

They made their way back along an incredibly narrow corridor, past the restrooms. Max peeked inside and saw there was a very old rusted tin bath just lying there. He pointed it out to Luke.

"Did you know Churchill would occasionally take meetings from his bath? He'd also dictate letters to his secretary from the comfort of the water as she sat outside. Wonder if he ever bathed in that one?"

"Why don't you ask Patrick? Wouldn't surprise me if he was best buds with Churchill."

"That's not a bad idea. Remind me to do that later."

"Of course. It's not like I've got anything else on my mind at the moment."

They found a supply room, and Max loaded their backpacks with equipment, drinks, and snacks. There was also a wardrobe full of clothes of assorted sizes. Max searched through it, found some black jeans, a black long-sleeved top and a black jacket, and handed them to Luke.

"Put these on," he said.

Max found the same for himself and changed into his new clothes. Although they looked like regular clothes at a glance, they were covered in a strange material.

"What is this?" Luke asked, rubbing his hand across it.

"No idea. Patrick and Carter designed them. It's supposed to impede security cameras, making it difficult for them to pick the wearer up. Probably wise we wear them, don't you think?"

"Sounds good to me."

They were a perfect fit for both and felt comfortable and warm.

"Right. That should do it."

"So," said Luke. "Let's go and break into one of the world's most famous museums and steal us a dragon's tooth."

There was a pause before both burst out laughing. Together, they began walking up the 122 steps to make their way out of Down Street Station.

26

"**I**s Luke okay?"

"He's absolutely fine, Sarah. He's with Max, who's also keeping well and the pair of them are currently regrouping in Down Street tube station. However, there's been a development. It would appear there is another tooth at the Natural History Museum. They're on their way there now to claim it before other parties do so. Once they have gained the tooth, they will head to Stonehenge for the eclipse, which is where we shall meet them, once we make our way out of here."

Startling them all, an alarm klaxon began its continuous call.

"Time's up!" yelled Serge. "Quick. This way!"

They ran across the courtyard towards another building that was housing military trucks, jeeps, cars, and motorbikes. It was similar in size to an aircraft hangar.

"Shoot the tyres on as many vehicles as you can, as quickly as you can," instructed Carter.

The four of them began firing their weapons, with

Patrick nearly losing his balance as the powerful gun bucked in his hands.

"Head for the middle. You'll know the Beast when you see it," said Serge.

They continued shooting at as many modes of transport as they could as they made their way to the centre. Sitting there was the Beast. And it absolutely was a beast. It looked like a Monster Truck, but its wheels were smaller and in proportion with its body. It was a smooth, gun-metal grey colour and looked like it could withstand a lot of damage.

Outside the building, soldiers were massing and yelling at each other in German. They would be upon them in moments.

"Carter, you're driving. I need to open the gates for our escape," said Serge, who threw him the keys and dashed to the other side of the building to a console and began typing numbers into a computer.

Carter moved to the driver's side and opened the door. The inside was a mixture of military and luxury with plush leather seats and numerous switches and buttons. If Carter was daunted by all this technology, he didn't show it. He started the engine and it gave a powerful, yet somehow quiet growl. Patrick climbed inside as Sarah hung half in and half out, firing her gun at the approaching soldiers. The reinforced gates that acted as the entrance and exit to the building slowly began to slide apart.

"You need to go!" Serge shouted above the din of bullets. "Now!"

Carter did so, and the Beast began moving. Serge started to run after it, but just as he did, a bullet clipped his leg and he fell to the floor. He began crawling towards the others.

"No!" shouted Sarah, and she jumped out of the Beast to run and help him. Carter brought the jeep to a stop. The

German soldiers were advancing and Sarah realised she wouldn't be able to reach Serge in time. Carter was hanging out of his window, firing at the soldiers, but there were too many of them.

"Sarah! Get back in. You can't save him," Carter screamed.

"I have to try," Sarah said, but she knew Carter was right. She locked eyes with Serge, who understood what was going to happen.

"Go," he mouthed. Then more loudly, "Go! They'll close the gates. Leave now!"

Sarah nodded. "I'm sorry," she said and turned to run back to the Beast, climbing into the passenger seat next to Carter. Carter slammed his foot down on the accelerator and the armoured jeep's tyres burned rubber on the concrete floor and sped towards the gates.

As Serge had said, he was quickly overwhelmed by soldiers, and one of them had gone straight to the console to close the doors. They stopped moving outwards and slowly began to slide together once again. The Beast was still about 50 metres away, but gathering speed. It was going to be tight. Bullets were pinging harmlessly off the reinforced armour of the jeep, and even the wheels seemed to be protected.

"Carter, I know this is called the Beast, but if you don't get us through those doors, it'll be beastly for us," said Patrick.

"I'm trying, I'm trying."

Carter's foot was flat to the floor, and The Beast was moving faster and faster, but the gap between the doors was getting smaller and smaller.

"Everybody breathe in!" yelled Carter as the Beast thundered towards the doors. They blasted through the gap with an inch to spare either side and shot out into the German woodland. There was a wire fence running along the perimeter of the fortress which the Beast smashed through as though it weren't there.

"Well, they don't come much closer than that," said a relieved Carter, "but if this thing doesn't have a sat-nav, then we're in big trouble."

Aunt Sarah began pressing buttons on a monitor in front of her.

"Give me a moment," she said. "Here we go."

Aunt Sarah had changed the language on the display screen from German to English.

"Patrick? Where are we going?"

"Head for the centre of Berlin. I need to make a phone call."

As Sarah, Carter and Patrick drove off into the night, Sebastian had promptly arrived back in the hangar and was assessing the carnage. Only a handful of vehicles remained usable, but he ordered his men to stand down. Serge was still lying on the floor, clutching his wounded leg. Sebastian approached and stood over him.

"Obergefreiter Gruber. You are a traitor to our cause and will be punished accordingly."

"I was a dead man, anyway. Do your worst."

"My worst? Careful what you wish for, Gruber. Tell me, do you know the whereabouts of Luke Stevens?"

Serge tried to keep his face neutral, but Sebastian was an expert at reading micro-expressions, the minuscule reactions that people couldn't help but reveal when they were asked a question.

"I see you do. This is good news. Soon *I* shall know and we can continue as originally planned." he gave one last contemptuous look at Serge and gestured to a soldier. "Take

him to my office and prepare him for questioning immediately."

Serge was manhandled away as Sebastian looked on. It
didn't take long to break him. After just a few minutes, he
had told Sebastian everything he'd heard during his time
with The Guardians. Something he had said earlier also,
sadly, came true. After leaving Sebastian's office, Obergefreiter Serge Gruber was never heard from again.

27

"It's a thirty-minute walk from here to the Natural History Museum," said Max.

"But what do we do when we get there?"

"I have an idea, but it involves a tremendous amount of luck."

"I'm pretty sure we've used up all our luck."

"Well, let's hope it holds for a little while longer."

They were back on Piccadilly, heading towards the museum. Although it wasn't as busy as before, there were still a decent number of tourists and revellers. They kept their heads down, but maintained a watchful eye over those people around them, just in case Sebastian's soldiers had somehow tracked them down again.

"So, do you want to tell me what we're going to do, or do I have to guess?" Luke asked.

"We're going to walk in through the front door."

"You what?"

"Exactly that. I'll create a distraction to the side of the museum, which will draw off the security guards. We'll then jump over the iron gate and I'll open the front door."

"But those gates are huge. We've got no chance."

"I don't mean the red gate at the front. Just off from those, the gate becomes black and is only waist height. That's where we'll go in."

"And what about the guards?"

"We'll set off a small explosive smoke grenade to the side of the main building. There won't be any fire, so we don't have to worry about the Fire Brigade turning up. It'll just be smoke."

"Surely that will be enough to make the guards call the Fire Brigade, though?"

"I'm hoping that when they reach the affected area, most of the smoke will have gone and they'll investigate it themselves. By then, we'll already be inside. I have a special corrosive substance that will eat through the wooden door in seconds."

"How on earth are you carrying that?"

"It's in a plastic container which doesn't affect it. It only becomes active once it's in contact with wood."

"If you say so, Max."

"I don't, Patrick does. I find it best not to ask questions about his inventions. You do know exactly where we need to go, don't you?"

"Yes. The tooth is on display in the dinosaur section. I guess that's what they think it most closely resembles. It's near to the main entrance hall."

"Good. We'll be in and out and heading to Stonehenge before you know it."

"You know, an awful lot of this could go wrong."

"That's the spirit, Luke. Nice and positive." Max rolled his eyes.

The rest of the journey to the museum was made in

silence, both focused on the risky business ahead of them. They turned onto Cromwell Road and saw the majestic building in front of them taking a moment to appreciate the sheer spectacle of it before Max purposefully moved off, with Luke following him. The road was quiet, with only a few pedestrians about. Traffic was busier, with the familiar sight of London's red double-decker buses making frequent appearances.

Max took his backpack off, reached into it and pulled out a small, round metallic object as well as two Tupperware containers that were housing what looked like grey play-doh.

"After I throw this grenade, we need to get over the gate as quickly as we can. When we reach the door, smear this onto it just above where I'll spread mine. It doesn't need to be a large hole, but big enough for us both to fit through. You'll go in first and I'll follow your lead. Questions?"

"Several, but let's not waste time. Let's go."

Max took a quick look around him, pulled the pin from the smoke grenade, and let it fly. It landed to the side of the museum, down what looked like an alleyway, and immediately began to release its smoky load. Max and Luke quickly jumped over the black gate and stealthily made their way towards the entrance. They crouched down behind a stone wall when they heard the squawk of a radio and the sound of footsteps near them. It was a security guard on his way to check out the smoke.

Once he had passed, Max and Luke ran towards the doors. Stooping down, they opened the containers and promptly began coating the door with the contents. Luke had no idea what was about to happen and was amazed to see the surface of the substance bubbling and making a quiet hissing sound. Although it was an incredibly thick wooden door, Patrick's creation made quick work of it. A hole now appeared where the substance had been placed, large enough for them to fit through individually, which they did.

"Man, that stuff's pretty toxic," whispered Luke. "Patrick's certainly got some wacky ideas."

"Focus, Luke. Let's get in and get out."

"Right you are."

They moved into the main hallway where the once imposingly wonderful sight of 'Dippy the Dinosaur' had hung from the ceiling, replaced now with an equally impressive skeleton of a Blue Whale.

"It's left here," said Luke.

They turned into a corridor and made their way to the Blue Zone, the dinosaur section of the museum. On entering, they were greeted by several dinosaur skeletons suspended from the ceiling above them. They kept their eyes focused on the many display cases scattered around the room.

"You take left, I'll go right," Luke instructed.

Max quickly scanned the numerous teeth on display. Tyrannosaurus, Velociraptor, Iguanodon, Scolosaurus and Triceratops were just some he could see, but nothing of unknown origin.

"Max. We're in trouble," hissed Luke.

Max ran to him and immediately understood why. There was a piece of glass missing from the top of the display case, perfectly cut with what must have been a precise, high-tech device. A piece of paper that stated 'tooth of unknown origin' wasn't showcasing a tooth. In its place was a book. The book that Luke had used to thwart Erich. The Nazis had beaten them to it.

Max and Luke looked at each other, disappointment written on their faces. They didn't have time to dwell on that, though. With a piercing shriek that made them both jump, the museum's alarm went off.

"Run!" shouted Max.

Luke did exactly that.

28

After Sebastian had extracted the information he needed from Serge, he began preparations for the next part of his plan. He was holding a clipboard and issuing orders to some of his troops when Felicity approached him.

"Stonehenge? I've always wanted to go there."

"Alas, Felicity, your visit must wait for another time."

"Why? I don't understand."

"I have a job for you."

"But I want to see this through. I deserve that much."

"Patience, Felicity. You will get what's coming to you once we have fulfilled the Prophecy."

Felicity detected an edge to Sebastian's voice which unsettled her.

"What do you want me to do?"

"As you might already be aware, shortly before the end of the war, several high-ranking members of the Nazi party made their way to South America, in particular Argentina. Once there, they integrated themselves into society with new identities. A fresh start, so to speak. Many started families and I am in possession of an exclusive list of those that have remained loyal to our cause ever since. I need you to send a secure communication to these brave soldiers to prepare them for what will follow once we are successful in our quest. Meanwhile, the rest of us shall make our way to Stonehenge to reclaim our rightful position as the head of the New World Order. Do not let me down, Felicity."

"Have I ever?"

"Not yet. But there is always a first time. And I know you don't need reminding of the penalties should you fail, yes?"

Felicity didn't think it wise to point out Sebastian's recent failures when it came to capturing Luke Stevens, so instead she fixed him with an icy stare.

"I understand your disappointment, but this is vital to our cause. Everything you need is here. You know where the communications centre is." Sebastian handed her the clipboard, smiled and walked away leaving Felicity to stew in silence.

Glancing at the list, Felicity was surprised to see a handful of surnames she recognised as perpetrators of some of the most despicable war crimes in history along with their new names. Anger rose within her as she contemplated her next move.

Felicity removed the list from the clipboard, folded it and placed it in her pocket. Instead of heading towards the communications centre, she walked in the same direction Sebastian had. She assumed Sebastian was heading towards one of the barracks to ready his men. She was right. She made her way across the courtyard and entered the barracks, keeping to the shadows at the back of the room. Sebastian was addressing his troops, explaining their next move.

Once he had finished, he left his men to change into the

appropriate uniform for the next stage of their operation. As they did so, Felicity continued to embrace the darkness, timing her moment. Once the soldiers were dressed, Felicity strode purposefully into the room whilst scanning the many bodies present. She selected one and approached him.

"Excuse me, but are you Obergefreiter Brehme?"

If the soldier was surprised to see Felicity, he didn't show it.

"No, Fraulein, I am Obergefreiter Brühl."

Felicity consulted her clipboard.

"Ah, yes. Obergefreiter Brühl. You must come with me at once. Your skills are requested by the highest authority for a secret mission."

"Me? Are you sure?"

"Do not question me, Obergefreiter Brühl. Herr Hitler would be most displeased to learn of your lack of respect for his authority."

Obergefreiter Brühl gulped and nodded his head.

"Follow me." Felicity discreetly led him back the way she had come. Once they were in the shadows, she dropped her clipboard to the floor. Obergefreiter Brühl automatically bent down to pick it up for her and as he did, Felicity quickly spun around him and removed his pistol from its holster in one fluid movement. She was so fast that Obergefreiter Brühl hadn't even noticed. When he stood up and realised Felicity wasn't there, he blinked in confusion. Before he had time to turn around, Felicity had clubbed him on his head with the butt of the gun and he dropped to the floor as if he were made of jelly.

Felicity managed to drag him deeper into the shadows and began to strip him of his uniform. Quickly discarding her own, she put on the dark clothes which, luckily for her, included a face mask. They were slightly too big, but would pass a brief inspection.

Holstering the pistol and taking a deep breath, Felicity ran towards the departing soldiers and subtly joined their ranks at the back. She would be going to Stonehenge after all.

29

Carter, Sarah and Patrick had driven through the countryside and were heading into the centre of Berlin. Their journey had been a quiet one, which concerned Carter.

"They didn't come after us. Surely we didn't destroy all their vehicles?"

"It's possible," Patrick replied. "There were a lot of bullets flying about."

"I don't like it. It was too easy. We need to be prepared for some kind of retaliation."

Carter looked over at Sarah and saw she was deep in thought. Patrick noticed too.

"Serge was an incredibly brave young man, Sarah. There was nothing you could have done," said Patrick.

"I know. But he looked so scared at the end. He knew what Sebastian would do to him."

"That reminds me. We must assume that poor Serge told Sebastian everything he'd heard about the extra tooth and the Natural History Museum. I must phone Max to warn them."

He used the satellite phone to call him, but there was no answer.

"They must be busy. I'll try again later."

"What's waiting for us in Berlin, Patrick?" Carter asked.

"Somebody I haven't seen for a very long time," he answered sadly.

Patrick didn't expand on this, and Carter knew better than to ask him for more details. Instead, Patrick had retreated into himself and was staring sorrowfully outside his window. Carter continued driving the powerful car towards Berlin. The countryside began to turn into smaller towns before later revealing larger buildings that were home to Germany's capital city.

As they arrived in the centre, Patrick directed Carter to an expensive-looking apartment block.

"Head for the garages, Carter," Patrick instructed.

The garages were all numbered, and Patrick told him to approach number 11. Carter reversed towards it ("in case we need to leave quickly") and was surprised to see it open upon his approach.

"She's watching us," Patrick said.

Carter and Sarah shared a curious look. They exited the Beast and noticed that the garage hardly had anything in it. There were workbenches and shelving units, but all were empty. A discreet keypad on the back wall caught their attention, which made them think that there was much more to this room than met the eye. They walked towards some steps at the back of the garage, which ended at a door. Walking through, they entered a short corridor that finished at a solid wooden door.

"Aren't you going to knock?" asked Sarah.

"No need. She knows we're here, and I imagine is making us wait deliberately. It's the sort of thing she'd do."

They waited and waited until Patrick's impatience reached its threshold, and he went to knock. Just as he was about to, the door opened inwards and they were greeted by a formidable elderly woman with a scowl on her face. The lady stared at Patrick with a ferocious intensity. She turned her back on her three visitors and walked inside her flat.

"I do enjoy a warm welcome," Carter whispered.

"It was warmer than I expected," Patrick whispered back.

They walked inside, Aunt Sarah closing the door behind her.

Although it was a large apartment, it was minimalistic. A few pieces of art hung on the walls, some of which Sarah recognised, others she didn't. Walking past the kitchen, she noticed the work surfaces were bare, just like in the garage. They followed the lady into a living room that had a table, two sofas and a reclining armchair. Carter looked, but couldn't see a television, which unsettled him. She didn't invite them to sit down.

"Well?" she said, staring directly at Patrick, her arms folded.

"Maria, may I introduce my good friends, Sarah and Carter?"

"I don't care who they are. What. Do. You. Want?"

Patrick sighed. "I'm sorry we're barging in on you like this, but it's time. The Chosen One has the tooth, and the eclipse is tomorrow. We need your help to get to Stonehenge before it's too late."

The lady continued to stare at Patrick, her face remaining impassive. She then approached and slapped him across his face so fast that Carter and Sarah hadn't seen it coming.

"No," she said, and walked out of the room.

"Patrick?" asked Sarah. "Who is that?"

"That," he replied, rubbing his face, "is my wife."

30

L uke and Max ran in silence back towards the main
entrance, their feet slapping on the wooden floor.

"Oi!" came a voice from behind them. Luke
turned and saw a security guard some 50 metres away. He
began to speak into a walkie-talkie as he chased after them.
Max brought his rucksack around and fumbled inside it. He
pulled out another smoke grenade, removed the pin, and
dropped it behind him. Quickly, the hall began to fill with
smoke, making it difficult for the guard to see in front of
him.

Luke and Max reached the door and ducked through the
hole they had made earlier. They could hear raised voices
and the occasional beep of a radio, but couldn't see any
more guards.

"Follow me," said Max.

They ran into the courtyard, following the way they had
entered the grounds of the museum. They hid behind a wall
and reassessed their situation. Several security guards ran
towards the main entrance, and the smoke was now starting
to waft through the hole.

"Let's go back over the gate and away from here," urged Max.

They kept low and ran back towards the gate and leapt over it.

"Take your jacket off and turn it inside out," Max said.

They both did so, and Luke was surprised to see that it was reversible. The black material was now grey and altered their appearance enough to not warrant the attention of anyone looking for two people dressed all in black.

"Well, that didn't quite go as planned," said Luke, catching his breath.

"It does rather complicate things. Let's get further away and then I can call Patrick."

"Erich and the others must be near. How the hell did they know about the tooth?"

"I imagine something happened to Patrick, Carter, and your aunt in Germany. That or Patrick's new friend Serge wasn't as friendly as they'd first thought. Damn it! It's my fault. If I'd listened to you and not mentioned that damned second tooth, we wouldn't be in this mess. For what it's worth, I'm sorry. Either way, Sebastian will have the tooth soon and that is not good for anyone. Keep your eyes peeled. The last thing we need is to get jumped by Erich and lose the other tooth. I'd expect they wouldn't risk attacking us and potentially losing what they've just gained, but you never know."

"Are we heading back to the car?"

"Yes."

"Good. Then we can check on Séamus and Pamela. Make sure they're okay."

"Good idea."

They walked back to St James's Square and the London Library. In the distance, they could hear the wail of several sirens. They might be heading for the Natural History Museum, Luke thought, but in a vast city like London, anything could happen at any time. Their car was still parked where they'd left it. They walked past it and up the steps to the entrance. Peering in through the glass panels on the door, they could see Séamus and Pamela sitting down with cups of tea beside them. Max knocked and waved at them. Séamus gingerly stood up, using his cane, and went to let them in.

"Séamus, thank goodness you're both alright," said Max.

"We're fine. Those Nazi fools gave us both a crack on the noggin, but we're grand."

They moved inside and greeted Pamela.

"Pamela, I'm so sorry you've been dragged into this," said Max.

"It's quite nice to have a bit of excitement in my life, for once," she smiled. "Séamus explained the situation to me. It sounds awfully exciting although perhaps that's just the mild concussion talking."

"What happened?" asked Luke.

"They had guns. They tied me up and waited for Pamela to return. When she did, the cowards threatened to shoot her. I had no choice but to take them down to the vault and show them where you had gone and tell them what you had taken. I'm sorry."

"You have absolutely nothing to apologise for, Séamus," Max assured him. "You did the right thing and I would have done the same under those circumstances. Anyone would."

Séamus nodded his thanks and checked the cut on Pamela's head. He had applied a few stitches to it using the library's first aid kit.

"Did they catch up with you?" Séamus asked.

"They did at Green Park station, but we escaped," Luke answered. "However, they took something we needed from the Natural History Museum. Now we need to get to Stonehenge before the eclipse tomorrow evening."

"You both look exhausted," said Séamus. "You need some rest before you go. We can improvise some beds right here in the offices. We have plenty of cushions and it's warm enough to not get cold."

"He's right, Max. We've been at it for ages without proper rest. Something tells me we'll need to be on top form for whatever happens tomorrow."

Max frowned, but nodded his head.

"Okay. Thank you. First, I need to make a call to Patrick and let him know the Nazis now have a tooth."

At the mention of Patrick's name, Séamus went to say something but stopped himself. Instead, he shuffled off towards Pamela.

"Pamela, we'll get some sleep here, too, and then the four of us can leave together in the morning before the first shift starts. They can drive you home and then I'll go with them to Stonehenge."

"You must be joking. I'm not leaving you now, Séamus. You saved my life. Besides, I need to make sure you come back from Stonehenge so I can make you a nice dinner."

Séamus flushed red, and the two gave each other a nervous smile that turned into a relaxed laugh. Luke didn't know what to do and so gave an awkward cough.

"Ahem. So, err, about this bed?"

"Of course, Luke. This way." Séamus took Luke into one of the offices. "You can use this sofa. Should be comfortable enough."

"Thanks, Séamus."

Luke took one last look into the library, where Max had the satellite phone to his ear. The moment he put his head down and closed his eyes, he fell asleep.

31

"**E**x-wife!" came a shout from another room.

"We're not divorced, Maria."

"We bloomin' well should be!"

Patrick looked sheepishly at Sarah and Carter. Neither of them knew what to say. Maria came back into the room carrying a cardboard box. She threw it to the floor rather unceremoniously.

"This is yours. You can take it when you leave."

"Maria, we need to talk."

Just then, Patrick's satellite phone began to ring. He took it out and went to answer it.

"Typical," said Maria. "There's always something more important than talking to me. This is the story of my life."

"Max?"

Patrick listened carefully to what Max had to tell him about the tooth being taken by Erich. He explained they were with Séamus and were going to get some much-needed sleep before beginning their journey to Stonehenge in the morning.

"You're with Séamus now?" Patrick glanced at Maria as he said this. She stared impassively back at him. "I see. Yes, we're all fine here. Well, my cheek's a little sore, but I probably deserved that. Well, look after each other and we'll hopefully see you at Stonehenge tomorrow."

He ended the call and spoke to Sarah and Carter.

"Luke and Max are fine. They're with my brother and his friend at the London Library where they're going to recharge their batteries before travelling to Stonehenge tomorrow. Unfortunately, they failed to retrieve the tooth in time. Sebastian now has it which has possibly levelled the playing field." He turned to Maria. "Maria, please. You have to help us get to Stonehenge."

"Why?" she asked.

"Why? You know why. The prophecy will be fulfilled tomorrow. The Guardians need to band together to help Luke, the Chosen One. Sebastian now has a tooth and could still be victorious. It's your duty to make sure that doesn't happen."

"My duty? Don't make me laugh. I gave everything to the Guardians. Everything. And you threw it in my face."

"Shall we leave you both to it?" Carter asked awkwardly.

"You stay right where you are, young man," snapped Maria. "I want you to hear what this old weasel has to say."

"Maria," Patrick began.

"Tell them. If you don't, I will."

Patrick shuffled and looked from Maria to Sarah, back to Maria, and then to Carter. Sarah had never seen him look so old and small. He gave a nervous cough and began to speak.

"I, ahem. I thought Maria and my brother were, well, were, you know..."

"Having an affair," Maria finished for him. "After everything we'd been through over the years. You didn't trust me. Did our marriage vows mean nothing to you? Because they certainly meant something to me."

"It's your duty as a Guardian to help."

"My duty? Stuff my duty, you old fool."

The pair stared at each other.

"Maria, I'm sorry. It's something I've regretted every day since –"

"Since what? Since you left me? You can't even say it. You're pathetic."

Sarah and Carter were stunned.

"Please, Maria. This is bigger than me. Than you, than us. The Guardians have been waiting for this moment for centuries. The time has come and evil might still be victorious. You need to put your feelings for me aside for 24 hours and help us."

They continued to look at each other.

"I'm so sorry." Patrick began to sob. "My stupid pride prevented me from reaching out. But I'm here now and I'm sorry. I'm so sorry."

"You're here because you need me."

"Yes. I need you. In more ways than one."

After a minute, her expression softened. She crossed the room to stand in front of him and looked deeply into his eyes.

"Stupid, stubborn fool," she whispered.

"If you're going to hit me again, please do so on the other side of my face. I think you made one of my teeth loose on this side earlier."

Maria couldn't help but laugh, and the two of them embraced. Although Sarah and Carter were rather perplexed at the scene that had just played out in front of them, they couldn't help but smile at their reunion. As Maria pulled away from Patrick, she took his hand.

"What do you need?" she asked.

32

Max woke Luke up at 7 am with a rough shake to the shoulder.

"I'm awake. Leave me alone," he grunted.

"Good morning to you, too, Chosen One. Come on. We can freshen up in the staff bathroom before getting some breakfast."

Luke didn't feel hungry at all as his thoughts instantly strayed to this evening's lunar eclipse and whatever lay ahead of him. It would seem having to save the world made you lose your appetite.

Leaving his temporary bedroom, he greeted Séamus and Pamela, who both looked a lot better than they had the previous night. After brushing his teeth and having a quick wash, Luke was feeling more human. Pamela had made tea for everyone, and they sat reviving themselves with the hot drink.

"Pamela, I think you should reconsider coming. It's going to be dangerous, and we've all been preparing for this moment for a long time," urged Max.

"I understand Max and all this talk of dragons and special powers is a lot to take in, but just you try to stop me. I grew up in the East End and we got battered by those Nazi brutes for months. I know they lost the war, but I lost my father to them. And after what they did to us last night, if I can help in even the tiniest way, then I'm in."

Séamus beamed at her, and Luke was impressed by her steely determination.

"Very well. We'll explain more about what's happening on the way. It should only take a few hours to get there."

"Will we be going straight to Stonehenge?" asked Luke.

"I think we should. We can blend in with the tourists and assess the situation unless Patrick has another plan."

"Sebastian might have the same idea."

"He might, but that's a chance we'll have to take. We'll stop to get some food on the way. You should never go into battle on an empty stomach."

"I don't think I can eat anything, Max," said Luke.

"Nonsense. Some greasy rashers of bacon and oily fried eggs will sort you right out."

Luke's face turned pale at the thought. He excused himself and ran to the bathroom to throw some cold water on his face. He looked at his reflection and thought about how his life had changed over just a few days. His very existence had been turned upside down and there he was, a 13-year-old boy with the fate of the world on his shoulders. His thoughts turned to his parents.

"I wish you were here to help me."

As he said that, the tooth around his neck began to glow hotter than ever. Luke reached up to hold it and closed his eyes. His mind exploded with images of his mum and dad, snapshots of his short life with them colliding in a beautiful avalanche. Luke knew exactly what it meant, and he felt comforted.

Whilst Luke was freshening up, Pamela addressed Max.

"How old is that young man?"

"He's just turned 13."

"Just turned 13," she repeated, and gave Max a stern look. "Not even close to being an adult, and here he is with a burden he shouldn't have to bear. Perhaps consider how he's feeling right now before you talk about such frivolous things as bacon and eggs. Is it you that has the fate of humanity in their hands?"

Max swallowed and looked down at his feet.

"No, it isn't," he mumbled.

"No, it isn't," Pamela once again repeated. "Do better, Max, and have some empathy."

"Yes, Pamela. I'm sorry." Max was suitably embarrassed.

Séamus couldn't keep the smile from his face.

Luke walked back into the library and noticed a slight tension in the air.

"Is everything alright?" he asked.

"Of course it is, Luke," answered Pamela. "How are you feeling?"

"I'm much better now. Thanks for asking."

"Pleased to hear it, dear." She shot Max a look.

"Luke, you don't need to worry about food. If you're not hungry, that's fine. We'll be led by you on this and I'm sorry if I was a little, um, inconsiderate and, well, stupid earlier."

"How much earlier? From when we first met or just now?"

Max looked stung by Luke's words. "Well, I meant just now, but I suppose I was also a bit of a prat when we first met too."

"Don't worry about it, Max. It's fine. Believe it or not, I've enjoyed our time together. Shall we?"

Together, the four of them left the library and climbed into Max's car. Luke didn't know what to expect when he got to Stonehenge, but he knew one thing. He wasn't alone.

33

Patrick, Sarah, and Carter had spent the night at Maria's house. Maria had used her own room, Sarah the guest room, whilst Patrick and Carter had to make do with sharing a sofa-bed. Between Carter's tremendous bulk and Patrick's snoring, the pair both struggled with sleep. It was also about 7 am when Maria woke them and began to prepare breakfast.

"I wonder what Luke's doing now?" mused Sarah. "It seems strange that we're here having breakfast when we all know what we're up against later this evening."

"Well, this is the problem. We *don't* know," answered Patrick. "Sadly, we have no way of knowing exactly what Luke and ourselves will be facing. We need to be ready for all eventualities."

Patrick and Maria had spent most of the evening making phone calls, whilst Aunt Sarah and Carter had loaded up on weapons from Maria's private stash.

"Like any great city, Berlin's not always the safest place to live," had been her response when Carter's eyes bulged out of his sockets at seeing the small arsenal in front of him.

"How are we going to get all this stuff to Stonehenge?" asked Carter.

"I have some friends in high places, Carter," said Maria. "It won't be a problem."

Carter raised his eyebrows.

After they had finished breakfast, they carried their equipment down to Maria's garage. Carter loaded up the Beast and went to get in with Sarah, who took the passenger seat next to him. Patrick opened one of the back doors.

"Where do you think you're going?" Maria asked.

Patrick gave her a questioning look. She held his gaze, and both began to smile.

"Don't tell me you still have it?" said Patrick.

"Of course I still have it, you old fool. I've even updated her."

She pressed a button on a key ring and a hidden panel on one of the side walls slid back to reveal a sight that brought tears to Patrick's eyes. It was a motorbike, but not just any motorbike. It was incredibly low to the ground, so much so that the person driving it would almost be lying down and although at first glance it looked old-fashioned, it had been modified with a futuristic finish. But what made it stand out was the bullet-shaped sidecar. Patrick went over and tenderly ran his hands over it.

"Oh, my. I've not seen her for so long. She looks magnificent."

"I thought you'd be pleased. Come on. Put these on and get into position."

Maria threw Patrick an all-in-one protective jumpsuit and had one for herself. They put them on over their clothes and then Maria passed him a helmet.

"Just like old times, eh?"

"This is wonderful, Maria. Just wonderful."

Sarah and Carter looked utterly perplexed at the sight of two people with a combined age of what must be over 160 getting kitted up to ride in one of the most powerful-looking motorbikes they'd ever seen. Patrick somehow manoeuvred himself into the sidecar whilst Maria straddled the seat.

Carter drove the Beast into the courtyard and was followed by Patrick and Maria, who pulled up alongside them.

"I drive fast and I drive hard," Maria said. "Ready?"

"But I don't know where we're going!" protested Carter.

"Well, you'd better keep up then!"

With that, the motorbike and sidecar combination sped away, leaving Sarah and Carter to splutter in disbelief. The last thing they heard was the sound of Patrick and Maria's laughter as they quickly faded into the distance.

"What are you waiting for?" said Sarah. "Go!" She too began to laugh as Carter put his foot down on the accelerator and the Beast lurched forwards.

"This isn't what I signed up for!" Carter was laughing too.

Maria wasn't kidding when she'd said she drove fast and hard. Carter had to use all his considerable driving skills to keep up, and twice he feared he'd lost them completely. Maria had rocketed towards the outskirts of Berlin, the opposite side of the city and away from where Carter, Sarah and Patrick had been held captive the previous day, until they arrived at a small, private airfield.

Maria had a quick word with a man in an official uniform who waved them through a set of gates and they drove into a hangar. They were greeted by a cheerful mechanic, who had been working on the small jet in front of them.

"Good morning, Maria!" he called out as they approached.

"Hans, how are you?"

"Can't complain, can't complain. Nobody to complain to, anyway," he laughed.

Hans and Maria shook hands.

"Hans, these are my friends Patrick, Sarah, and Carter. They'll be accompanying me on my journey today."

They all greeted each other with polite words and nods.

"Very good. She's all fuelled up and ready to go. May I help with the luggage?"

"Thank you, but that won't be necessary. We'll take it from here. Are we good to go now?"

"That's right. You have clearance to take off when you're ready."

"Splendid. Well, then. Tuscany, here we come." Maria gave Carter and Sarah a pointed look and headed up the steps and onto the plane. They followed, carrying their bags of weaponry. Once the steps leading to the plane had been pulled in and the door locked, Carter noticed they were the only four on board.

"Maria, where's the pilot?"

"You're looking at her."

"You?"

"Me. Why? Anything you want to say, young man?"

Carter had about a hundred questions, but kept them to himself.

"Just when you thought things couldn't get any stranger," he muttered to Sarah.

"Maria, why did you tell Hans we were going to Italy?" asked Sarah.

"Simple. I don't trust him. You never know who Sebastian has in his pocket, so I thought I'd try to throw him off our scent for a while. I filed a flight plan to Tuscany because in a small village there called Chiusdino lies the Sword in the Stone. I believe the prophecy mentions stones, yes?"

"Are you talking about King Arthur's sword in the stone?"

"No, my dear. We believe that to still be in Cornwall somewhere. This sword belonged to a wealthy Italian knight called Galgano Guidotti. He had a vision of the Archangel Michael and his sword was plunged into the ground to mark the spot where it happened. A chapel has since been built around it. Over the years, many people have attempted to steal it, which is why it is now protected by a Perspex shield. On a more sinister note, it's even surrounded by the mummified hands of those would-be thieves. Now, if you'd like to make yourselves comfortable and take your seats, we'll be off shortly. Patrick, you're with me."

"Coming, dear," Patrick said as he bounced along after Maria into the cockpit.

Sarah and Carter couldn't help but burst out laughing once the cockpit door had been closed. They kept their bags near them and sat down next to each other into leather seats and fastened their seatbelts. Patrick's voice came over a PA system into the cabin.

"*Ladies and gentlemen, this is your Captain speaking –*"

"*Don't be ridiculous, I'm the Captain. You're just the co-pilot and that's being generous. To tell you the truth, I don't need you here at all, but I wanted the company,*" interrupted Maria.

"*Okay, okay,*" Patrick said. "*This is your co-pilot speaking. Please make sure your seatbelts are fastened as we are about to make our way to the runway before we begin our quest to Stonehenge. Once the seatbelt sign has gone out, feel free to stretch your legs and to eat Maria's expensive food.*"

The plane gently taxied to the runway before exploding

forwards with such force that Sarah and Carter were pulled back into their seats. Not long after, the nose of the plane rose and the small jet began its journey to the ancient monument of Stonehenge.

34

They'd stopped for a quick breakfast at a roadside cafe on their way to Stonehenge. Luke had surprised everyone, himself included, by wolfing down a full English. Max's quip about the condemned man's last meal earned him a sore shin after Pamela had kicked him under the table.

Their journey towards Salisbury was surprisingly relaxing and Max had even let Luke choose the music. He'd wanted to please everyone, so chose the most non-offensive radio station he could think of, Classic FM. It had proved an excellent choice with its mix of old, classic composers and some contemporary artists thrown into the mix. They'd even played the *Star Wars* theme, which made Luke think of Charlie. Would he ever be able to tell him about this? Would Charlie believe him if he did? Luke smiled to himself as he imagined what Charlie's reaction would be if he told him about the last few days.

"We'll park up some distance away and wait to hear from Patrick. Sorry, Séamus, but there might be a bit of a trek involved," Max said.

"Don't patronise me, you pompous oaf!"

Luke burst out laughing. "That told you!" he said.

"My apologies, Séamus. I meant no offence."

"Offence is taken, Max. Just because one of my legs is useless it doesn't mean I can't kick you up the arse with it."

An awkward silence filled the car. Suddenly, Séamus exploded into peals of laughter, followed by Pamela and then Luke. Max was the last to join in, somewhat reluctantly.

It was mid-afternoon, and they had a long time to wait before the eclipse started. They found a place to park about two miles from the ancient site.

"Why Stonehenge? Why here?" Luke asked.

"Stonehenge has been surrounded in mystery for years and years," answered Pamela. "We may never know its true purpose. Many people believe it was used to study the movement of the sun and moon and that they had a certain power over their lives. Others think it was a place for healing. It's likely that ancient Britons held special ceremonies during days such as Midsummer's Day and Midwinter's Day. It might also have been used for funerals and is a burial ground. Either way, questions still hang over Stonehenge and there's mysticism to it that continues to baffle historians."

Their thoughts were interrupted by Max's satellite phone ringing. He answered it. "Hello?"

"*Max! How are you and the others?*"

"Patrick, we're all fine. We're in Salisbury a couple of miles from Stonehenge and waiting for you. I'll send you our exact position."

"*Splendid. We're on our way and should be with you in about an hour. I've booked us onto a Twilight Tour which will get us* nice and close to the stones for whatever is going to happen. How's Luke?"

"You can ask him yourself." Max passed the phone to Luke.

"Hi, Patrick."

"It's nice to hear your voice. How are you holding up?"

"I'm okay, considering I need to save the world and I have no idea what I'm supposed to do."

"That's the spirit. Well, don't worry. We're all here for you."

"How's Aunt Sarah?"

"She's fine. She's with Carter."

"Is she, now?"

Patrick chuckled. *"It's nice to see your aunt happy. We all need some happiness right now, so let's welcome it when it's found, hmm?"*

"I suppose so."

"Well, we'll be with you soon. Try not to worry. Remember, when times are dark, light can come from within."

"If you say so. See you soon. Bye."

Luke ended the call and handed the phone back to Max.

"I guess all we can do now, is wait," he said.

The four of them became lost in their thoughts. Luke closed his eyes and tried to relax. He drifted off to sleep and began seeing the most incredibly vivid dreams. He witnessed St George riding his horse, rescuing Florentia, and slaying the dragon. He caught glimpses of George's recovery and witnessed him voicing the prophecy. He saw the two children, Angelus and Victor, being born and watched snapshots of their growth flash in his mind. Luke dreamily watched Victor's descent into cruelty and the devastating effect it had on his family, his banishment and subsequent fury.

He then saw George on his deathbed and heard his last words, the very words Florentia had recorded. Then something unexpected happened. George turned his head and appeared to be gazing directly into Luke's eyes. He looked at peace and had a serene smile on his face. His smile widened as he continued to look at Luke. He then closed his eyes and silently passed away.

Luke woke with a start, surprised to see that it was evening. He was alone in the car, but could hear voices outside. The dream had felt so real. Luke felt fully awake and refreshed. He climbed out, stretched, and broke into a huge grin when he saw who was talking. Before he knew it, Aunt Sarah had wrapped both her arms around him and was hugging him like there was no tomorrow.

"You're crushing me, Aunt Sarah!" Luke wheezed.

"Sorry, it's just so good to see you."

"It's only been a day or so."

"True, but quite a lot has happened in that time."

"You're not wrong there."

Patrick and Carter greeted Luke warmly, and he was introduced to Maria. She gave Luke another bone-crunching hug and told him she was honoured to meet him. Luke had slept through the rather awkward reunion of Patrick, Maria, and Séamus. The trio had found a more private area, and a rather animated discussion ensued. There were tears from all three, which resulted in an embrace between all of them. Laughter followed, and they re-joined the others. The past would remain in the past and together, they would look to the future.

Patrick addressed the group. "So, here we are. Familiar faces, old friends and even new recruits. Welcome, all. We don't know exactly what we're going to be walking into, but whatever it is, we shall be together. We need to assume that

Sebastian and his soldiers will also be arriving soon or even already there. How many of them, I know not. There will be plenty of tourists, so hopefully, we can blend in if we separate into groups. I imagine Sebastian will do the same as even he wouldn't risk being seen in his full Nazi regalia and attacking dozens of tourists."

"How are we going to get away from Stonehenge's security, or even Sebastian? Don't forget that he also has a tooth now," Luke said.

"You leave the security to myself and Carter, young Luke. That isn't something you need to concern yourself with. Just, trust us."

"Whatever you say, Patrick," Luke answered, though he still had doubts.

"Right. Best foot forward, everyone. Even you, Séamus!"

Séamus clipped his brother around the ear, and the two moved off with their arms around each other. The others followed, with Aunt Sarah, Maria and Pamela forming a group, leaving Luke with Max and Carter.

"Max, do you mind if I have a quick word with Carter, please?"

"Of course not."

They continued walking together.

"In private."

"Oh. Yes, of course, I'll just catch up with the others."

Max did that, and Luke and Carter fell in step next to each other.

They walked in silence until Carter broke it.

"Something on your mind, Chosen One?"

"There are one or two things."

"Something other than saving the world?"

"Well, now that you mention it, yes."

"Would it involve your aunt?"

Luke remained silent.

"Luke, I've known your aunt for a very long time, and we've been through a lot together. A lot. She means everything to me. What are you worried about?"

Luke hesitated before answering. "Losing her. She's all I have left."

Carter digested these words carefully before replying.

"Luke, I'm not here to take her away from you. If she had to choose between you or me, she'd pick you and I'm okay with that. Your aunt is a remarkable woman, and I'm privileged to be part of her life. I'm also honoured to be part of yours, too. Whatever happens after this evening, whether it's good or bad, I need you to understand that I'd do anything for her, but also for you. Besides, if I ever upset you or your aunt, something tells me you'd use those new powers of yours to put me in my place."

"You'd better believe it."

The two laughed.

"Thanks."

"You got it."

"Have you got any advice for what's about to happen?"

"Me? Just be yourself and trust your instincts, is what I think. That's all any of us can do. And if things take a turn for the worst? Do whatever you can to make them better again."

"What if they don't get better?"

"At least you'll know you tried. Nobody can ask for more than that."

They quickened their pace to catch up with the others. Luke found his way to Aunt Sarah's side.

"You okay?"

"I am now. Listen, I just want to say thank you for the last few years. I can't have been the easiest person to have around and I want you to know that I appreciate everything you've done for me."

"What's brought this on?"

"Nothing. I should have said this to you a long time ago."

"Well, you're very welcome. You realise that just because you're the Chosen One, you still need to do the washing up when we get back home?"

Luke burst out laughing. "Fair enough. I also want to say that I like Carter."

Aunt Sarah turned to look at Luke. "What do you mean by that?"

"I'm not a kid, Aunt Sarah. I can see that you two are into each other and I just thought you should know that I think he's pretty awesome."

Aunt Sarah continued to look at Luke. Luke smiled at her.

"I think so too, Luke. Thank you."

Aunt Sarah put her arm around him and together they continued their walk to Stonehenge. Luke could see the enormous stones in the distance. It was an amazing sight. Luke captured the image in his mind; the stones, the sun beginning its slow descent for the day, and this unusual group of people that had made their way into his life. He could hear peals of laughter coming from the individual groups around him. Even Carter and Max were sharing a joke.

"Aunt Sarah?"

"Yes, Luke?"

"I'm glad we're all together."

Aunt Sarah held him even closer.

35

They arrived at the Visitor Centre, and Patrick showed a steward their tickets.

"Ah, you're just in time. The last bus to the site was about to leave. It's over there. Once you're on board, you can be on your way," the steward said.

"Keep your eyes peeled, everyone. We should stay in pairs. I'll be with Maria, Séamus with Pamela, Carter with Sarah, and Luke, you'll be with Max."

They boarded the coach, which was full of tourists, quickly scanning their faces for signs of Sebastian or his soldiers. They didn't recognise any of them, but they remained alert throughout the 10-minute journey to the stones.

They arrived, left the bus and broke off in different directions. Their tour guide ushered them towards the stones where there were several other tourists already looking at the magnificent sight. Luke couldn't help but be awestruck by the immense rocks around him. His mind boggled as he tried to imagine how the stones had been moved. The tour guide's information filtered through to him now and then. Some stones were 25 tons with the largest, the Heel Stone, about 30 tons.

There was a mystical air about the place as the twilight soaked the site in its amber light, giving it an ethereal glow. Looking up to the sky, Luke could see the full moon, its usual grey-white colour. Soon, that would change to a blood red. Luke couldn't help but shudder at the thought, and he began to feel nervous. Max followed Luke's gaze upwards.

"Amazing, isn't it? To think that the sun, Earth and moon will all be aligned together. A straight line. Under normal circumstances, we might even enjoy this."

Luke nodded in agreement. He had been scanning the crowds for any sign of Sebastian's men, but still couldn't see anyone that looked suspicious. What he noticed, however, was that there weren't any children present. And hardly any teenagers. Luke was probably the youngest there. He was just about to voice this observation to Max when he suddenly felt the hairs on the back of his neck and arms stand up.

"Max. Something's about to happen. I have that feeling again."

What came next happened quickly. There were noises from all around them, and several canisters landed amongst the groups of tourists and began spewing a dense white smoke. Max quickly recognised what it was.

"Tear gas. Sebastian's here. Stay close, Luke."

There were about a hundred people on the tour and all but Luke, Max, Aunt Sarah, Carter, Séamus, Maria and Patrick began to panic. Pamela was frightened as her eyes began to tear up uncontrollably. Séamus was doing his best to calm her, talking to her in soothing tones as he held her.

Max was coughing, and his eyes were also streaming,

making it impossible to see. He shouted to make himself heard above the shrieks of terrified tourists.

"Luke! Are you there?"

"I'm here, Max," and he took Max's arm. "It's not affecting me and I can see through the smoke."

"Of course you can," he spluttered.

Luke looked around him and began making out several shadowy figures some distance from the stones. They surrounded Stonehenge.

"Max, I can see about 30 people coming closer. We're surrounded and they've got guns."

The figures moved in and Luke could then see that they were all wearing gas masks. Several people stumbled towards them at different points, and the soldiers shouted at them and herded them back towards the centre of the stones. Luke continued scanning the advancing troops until his gaze settled on the one soldier who wasn't wearing a mask, even though the smoke was swirling all over him.

Sebastian was eyeballing Luke as he made his way towards him. He was smiling and walking with his usual swagger. As he got closer, Luke could see that around his neck and attached with a leather bond, just like his, was the second dragon's tooth.

The smoke began to clear, but people were still struggling to see properly. There was panic in the air, with several people crying in fear and from the effects of the tear gas. Occasionally, a scream could be heard. Sebastian addressed the scared and confused group.

"Ladies and gentlemen, good evening. First, I must apologise for interrupting your enjoyment of this magnificent site. If you cooperate and do exactly as I say, there will be no need to harm you and you will soon be on your way. If you do not cooperate, there will be consequences. Please, sit down."

The group did as he said.

"Except you, Luke."

Luke stood back up and faced Sebastian defiantly.

"How nice to see you again."

"Don't talk to me like we're Facebook friends, you utter berk."

"I suggest you keep a civil tongue in your mouth. It would be awful if something were to happen to your aunt."

Luke clenched his fists, but remained in place. He found Aunt Sarah in the crowd and saw that she was smiling at him, although she had tears streaming down her cheeks. Luke also found Carter, Patrick, Pamela and Maria, all wiping their faces, but looking at him with reassurance.

"The lunar eclipse is happening as we speak. Soon, the prophecy will be fulfilled and I shall rule all."

"I wouldn't count on that. Your lot have already tried to take over the world twice and look what happened there. Your not so great-granddad failed and so will you."

Sebastian gestured to two of his men, who lifted Aunt Sarah off the ground by her hair. Carter moved to step in but was kept in place by a soldier cocking his gun. Aunt Sarah was thrown against one of the stones where she hit her head and fell to the ground, unconscious.

"One more word, Luke. Just one more word and she will be gone," hissed Sebastian. "Take this one, him, the old man, and tie them up," Sebastian pointed out Max, Carter and Patrick. "The others are not a threat."

A small group of soldiers moved to take the three Guardians whilst the others kept their guns trained on the hostages on the ground. As the soldiers walked past Sebastian, one of them suddenly made a lunge for him, or rather, what was around his neck. Sebastian expected the move and easily stopped the soldier's hand mere centimetres from the tooth. He twisted the soldier's arm back behind his back. The soldier cried out in pain, a high-pitched yelp.

"I was wondering when you were going to make your move," Sebastian said as he ripped off the soldier's mask. It was Felicity.

"Felicity!" shouted Max.

He too was stopped from moving towards her by a soldier pointing their gun at him.

"Hi, Maxi. Having a nice evening?"

"It's just got a lot better!"

Sebastian himself tied Felicity's hands behind her back and pushed her towards a soldier who left her next to Aunt Sarah's slumped form. She was staring daggers at Sebastian.

"How long have you known?" she asked him.

"From the beginning. How I have enjoyed watching your little games. I particularly enjoyed your moment with Obergefreiter Brühl. That was most impressive. I do hope the poor boy woke up after you cracked his skull."

"I'm of the opinion one less Nazi in the world is a good thing. How did you know about that anyway?"

"Our security cameras are very discreet. I see everything. You have much to learn. You never stood a chance anyway. The tooth can only be removed by the person wearing it, and even then, only voluntarily. You may have fooled some of your friends, even your oafish husband, but you didn't fool me."

"Don't you dare talk about my husband like that. He's twice the man you are."

"To be fair, that isn't saying much when you consider he's a Nazi," said Max.

"You know what I mean, Maxi."

"I'm so incredibly proud of you, Felicity," Max beamed at her.

"Enough of this," shouted Sebastian. "Look!"

He pointed upwards to the moon, which was now coloured a breath-taking red. It looked wonderful. Whilst Sebastian was gaping at the spectacular sight above him, Patrick cried out one word.

"Now!"

Instantly, every one of the tourists stood up, each revealing a weapon that had been hidden under their clothes. They fanned out and aimed them at the soldiers, who had quickly realised they were outnumbered and were looking around in confusion. Max and Carter honed in on Sebastian, their guns aimed at his face. Séamus walked behind Sebastian and gave him an almighty kick on his bottom with his good leg.

"That's for giving me this limp!"

Sebastian smiled at Séamus. "It suits you, old man. Perhaps next time I will do something to your other leg." He turned his gaze on Patrick. "Those bullets will not hurt me," he mocked. "Like Luke, I have the power of the tooth with me."

"Ah, well, that's where you're wrong. These aren't ordinary guns and they don't fire ordinary bullets. You know my talents, Sebastian. I try to prepare for every occasion."

"You are bluffing."

"Would you like to take the chance?"

Sebastian remained where he was.

"Tell your men to drop their guns," ordered Patrick.

Sebastian did so, reluctantly.

"How did you do this?" he asked Patrick.

"Simple. I made a phone call. We've had people in place ready and waiting for this day for years, just in case. Every person here today, including those working, are Guardians."

As Sebastian digested this information, the Guardians rounded up the soldiers and tied them together in groups. Sebastian was about to respond when, suddenly, the ground beneath his feet began to vibrate. It shook so violently that they all struggled to keep their balance and had to put their arms out to steady themselves. A low rumbling could be heard, and it seemed to be gradually increasing in volume. High above them, lightning began to flash, with loud cracks of thunder following immediately after. The wind was howling all around them, dust and grass billowing and swirling in every direction. They raised their hands to protect their faces, and the noise was becoming too much to bear.

Then, after a spectacularly bright flash of lightning, an explosion ripped through Stonehenge. It wasn't like a bomb going off, and there wasn't any fire. It was like a concussive sound wave that swept through the site. Nearly everyone was blown off their feet and onto the floor. Once the wave had finished, all was immediately still and silent.

The dust cleared, and only two people were still standing right in the centre of the giant stones. Everyone else had been blown out of the inner circle. Stood in the middle and bathed in a strange light were Luke and Sebastian.

36

L uke tried to move his body, but couldn't. He could just about see outside the ring of light that surrounded him and saw Aunt Sarah, Carter, Patrick and the other Guardians lying motionless behind the stones. The only sound he could hear was his breathing and that of Sebastian's next to him.

"What is happening?" asked Sebastian.

Luke ignored him and concentrated on trying to move. He strained, but it was no good. An invisible force kept him firmly rooted to the ground. Luke calmed himself and focused on steadying his breath. From the corner of his eye, he could see Sebastian continuing his fight against whatever was holding him in place. He was sweating and veins were bulging in his neck.

The blood-red moon seemed to cast a beam of light directly onto Stonehenge. Mysterious particles were dancing within the glow, creating a mesmerising effect. Luke felt a euphoric sense of peace and tranquillity, quite a contrast to Sebastian, who was snarling and still fighting to move.

Luke could see a shadowy figure approaching from outside of the light, but he couldn't make out who or what it was. The closer it got, the larger it became. Luke could see that it was moving, almost cautiously, between the bodies lying prone outside of the circle. The figure made its way to the edge of the circle of light and stopped. Slowly, it began to move forward; the light illuminated its features, gradually revealing exactly what it was. Luke's breath caught in his throat, and even Sebastian had stopped straining.

It was a horse. Standing proud and striding into the inner circle, it was dazzling, pure white and draped in a caparison, a decorative cloth that covered its top half and part of its head. This was also white with a red stripe leading from the horse's nose to its tail, with another red stripe crossing the other in the middle. Sitting atop the horse and dressed with armour so polished it hurt to look at was a knight. His face was covered by a helmet that had a red and white feathered plume. In his left hand was a shield with the same colours, and strapped to his right side was a lance.

He brought the horse to a stop in front of Luke and Sebastian and remained seated. The knight clipped his shield to the horse's saddle and removed his helmet. He wore his salt and pepper hair long, and had a well-groomed beard. He appraised Luke and Sebastian with a curious gaze. When his eyes locked on Luke's, Luke was stunned. He was looking at the face he had seen in his recent dream. Here before him, somehow, was unquestionably the legendary St George.

"Luke Stevens. Wearer of the first tooth. It is a pleasure to meet you."

"Hello," Luke tentatively responded.

St George's voice was deep and resonant, but it had a softness to it. He had a slight accent, but Luke was too stunned to work out where it was from. St George then turned his gaze on Sebastian.

"Sebastian Hitler. Wearer of the second tooth. It is a pleasure to meet you."

Sebastian didn't speak.

"My name is Giorgio di Romano, but you will know me as St George. You both know the prophecy. You both know that a choice must be made. What happens next is up to you."

Luke went to raise his hand and was surprised to find that he was no longer held and could move freely. He gingerly lifted his arm. George looked at him.

"Luke?"

"Forgive me, St George. But, how is this happening? I mean, you died centuries ago. I don't understand. Sorry."

A ghost of a smile crossed St George's mouth. "The mysteries of the universe are complex, and I know not all the answers to the question you ask, Luke. I will share with you that which I know. Dragons were not supposed to survive for as long as they did. Dark magic and wizardry kept them alive age after age. However, where once they were controlled by those with power, they became too strong and broke free to threaten mankind's existence. As you are aware, after my battle with the dragon, I became infused with a power I could never fully understand and became haunted by visions. Some were a blessing, others a curse. Most I shared with my dear wife, Florentia, but some, I did not burden her with. I was shown dreams of what was once and what was to be. By whom, I do not know. Perhaps God, perhaps the Devil."

A look of surprise crossed Luke's face.

"Yes, Luke. They both exist. Alas, you cannot have one without the other. They have both shown their forms in many guises throughout the history of this planet. The balance of power is threatened regularly, and today, we find ourselves at another crossroads. You were both destined to be here on this night. You are both destined to make a choice, and that time is now."

Luke gulped and looked over at Sebastian. He was staring up at St George with a maniacal desire in his eyes, eager to hear what came next.

"I am ready!" Sebastian shouted. "I am ready to make my choice and to lead the New World Order."

"Very well," said St George. "The time has come."

St George climbed off his horse and stood in front of Luke and Sebastian. He raised his arms in the air, and both Luke and Sebastian instinctively closed their eyes. Time seemed to stand still. St George's voice spoke to them inside their minds at the same time. They could both hear what he was saying.

"Sebastian Hitler. You have a choice to make. Like your great-grandfather, you are an ambitious man. How far are you willing to go to see your dreams of the New World Order become a reality?"

"I will do whatever it takes!" screamed Sebastian.

"We shall see."

As St George said these words, Luke could see what Sebastian could see. There was a pretty blonde woman of Sebastian's age, gazing at a photograph in her hand and holding her belly with the other. She looked full of joy and excitement. She kissed the photograph, and as she brought it up to her lips, Sebastian and Luke could see what the image was. It was a scan of a baby. Sebastian's baby.

"To become the leader of your New World Order," continued St George, "you must sacrifice the life of your unborn child. If you do this, the world will be yours and your new age will begin. If you choose to spare the child's life, you and your soldiers will have the opportunity to start afresh. A new beginning for you and your family."

"Yes! I will do it!" Sebastian didn't hesitate. "Kill the child!"

Luke looked horrified. "Sebastian, no. Please, don't. It doesn't have to be like this," he begged.

"Be quiet, boy. Nothing shall stand in my way to get what I want. Nothing!"

Sebastian was hysterical, and his eyes burned with a ferocious intensity. St George's face remained neutral.

"Sebastian Hitler," St George was speaking again. "Is this your choice?"

"Yes, damn you. This is my choice. Make it so!"

"So be it. Please, give me your tooth to make your challenge complete."

Sebastian pulled the leather cord from around his neck and handed the tooth to St George.

"Luke Stevens. You have a choice to make. In your young life, you have known the pain of death and loss."

Luke and Sebastian could then see the same thing once again. It was Luke's parents. Snapshots of Luke's life played out before him. His parents looking at his hospital scan, his father's hands protectively around his wife's stomach. This quickly changed to other images. Luke's father holding a new-born Luke whilst his mother looked exhausted, but elated and full of love. Birthday parties, the first day of school, and Luke learning to ride a bike were all shown.

Luke watched his life unfolding and was enraptured. He then saw pictures of his parent's funeral and Aunt Sarah clutching him, tears rolling down their faces. Aunt Sarah bringing him to his new home, Aunt Sarah cooking him food, ironing his clothes and opening Christmas presents with him. This quickly changed to his parents once again, both looking right at him and standing in front of him. It was so real, Luke almost collapsed. His mother reached out to touch his cheek, and Luke gasped when he felt her touch. He could smell her hand, and memories flooded his mind. He began to weep tears of joy as well as tears of bitterness and anger.

"Luke. You can have your parents back and your life with them will start anew from this day. They will be alive and you will be a family once again, albeit in Sebastian's New World Order," said St George.

Luke couldn't believe what he was hearing.

"However, this comes at a price. The family you have left will cease to be. The Guardians, as they are known, that you have grown close to, will be no more. If you do not accept, you and the Guardians will suffer the consequences of life under Sebastian's New World Order. You must choose."

St George's words echoed in Luke's head and the image of his parents was still in front of him. They were smiling, and it made his heart ache. He was breathing rapidly and struggling to think clearly.

"Mum, dad," he whispered.

"Hurry, boy. Make your decision," snapped Sebastian.

Luke turned to look at him, but as he did, something behind Sebastian caught his eye. He could see Aunt Sarah, Carter, Patrick, Maria, Pamela, Séamus, Max and Felicity all lying unconscious beyond the circle of stones. He looked through the light and could see that Aunt Sarah and Carter were somehow holding hands. Maria had her head nestled on Patrick's chest, Séamus's head was resting in Pamela's lap, and Max and Felicity were wrapped in each other's arms. Luke smiled at the sight and knew instantly what he had to do. He turned to face his parents, took a deep breath, and sighed.

"Not yet," he whispered. Luke then looked at St George. "Thank you, St George, for the opportunity to have my parents back, but I must politely decline your kind offer."

"Luke Stevens. This is your choice?" asked St George with the hint of a smile.

"This is my choice. My family is already here with me. And my parents helped make that happen. This is the right thing to do."

"So be it. Please, give me your tooth to make your challenge complete."

Luke also pulled the cord from around his neck and handed it to St George.

"The choices have been made, and the end is nigh," St George announced.

"At last! The world is mine! The New World Order will cleanse the unclean and we shall rise stronger than ever!" Sebastian was triumphant.

"You'll still have to get through us. Even if we can't stop you, someone else will," Luke said defiantly.

St George watched this exchange with curious amusement.

"You fool! Did you not hear? I made my choice, you made yours and I win!"

"You're a monster. Sacrificing your own child? You truly are a Hitler."

Sebastian moved to strike Luke, but with a wave of his hand, St George stopped him in his tracks. Sebastian, once again, found that he couldn't move. He strained and fought, but he was stuck.

"You, Sebastian Hitler, have failed," St George said.

"What? I do not understand," spluttered Sebastian.

"You, Luke Stevens, have passed," St George smiled at Luke.

Luke looked confused.

"Good versus evil," continued St George, "and good will always triumph. This was a simple test. Sebastian, you failed. Your wife is not expecting your child, but you were not to know that. I am ashamed that we share a bloodline. To sacrifice an innocent child is truly evil, and you have proved yourself to be unworthy and the very worst of men. Luke, I'm sorry for putting you through that. You are an incredibly brave young man and I am proud that you have my blood running through your veins."

Luke considered St George's words.

"Angelus and Victor. Your sons. Victor settled in Germany," said Luke.

"You are correct, Luke. Whilst Angelus sided with good, Victor chose evil," he looked at Sebastian with disgust.

"What happens now?" Luke asked.

"Now, Sebastian must live with the consequences of his decision."

St George clicked his fingers. From the shadows of the stones rose black tendrils that wrapped themselves around Sebastian's body. He tried to scream, but his mouth was covered by the lengthy appendages. Sebastian managed to turn his head and looked at Luke, fear and desperation in his eyes. Luke wanted to help him, but St George put a hand on his shoulder.

"You cannot interfere, Luke. The prophecy must be fulfilled."

Sebastian's muffled cries pierced Luke's ears and he couldn't help but feel sorry for him as he was dragged away by whatever was gripping him. Closer to the stones he was pulled until, slowly, Sebastian was somehow sucked into one of the colossal rocks where he vanished, never to be seen again.

37

S ilence.

"I imagine you have many questions, Luke."

Luke let out a nervous laugh.

"One or two, St George."

"We have a short amount of time until the planets move out of alignment. Ask me what you will and, time allowing, I shall answer you."

Luke's brow creased in thought. "Okay. First, what the hell happened over the last few days? One minute I'm looking at paintings at the National Gallery with my friend Charlie, the next I'm humiliating the school bully, discovering my aunt leads a secret life protecting mankind from evil, a group of Nazis – including Hitler's great-grandson – are trying to kill me, I break into the Natural History Museum and now here I am talking to England's Patron Saint who just so happens to have been dead for about a million years! Seriously. Help me understand." The words tumbled out of Luke's mouth uncontrollably.

St George couldn't help but laugh. "Yes, it probably hasn't been the easiest few days for you, Luke. I know little, but I will share with you all that I can. It begins and ends with God and the Devil. There are those on the side of light and those that choose to walk in darkness. I was chosen to represent the light, just as you have been."

"But you could have chosen the dark?"

"Yes. Quite easily. It is the decisions we make that define us. Knowing wrong from right. Putting others before yourself. Taking the difficult option rather than the simple choice because you know, as you said, that it is the right thing to do. Sebastian was blinded by power and greed, just as his great-grandfather before him."

"Did you meet him? Adolf Hitler?"

"I did. He died not long after. He too chose poorly."

"What would have happened had I chosen to see my parents again?"

"That, I do not know. You may have been happy, but for how long? After all, it was the wrong choice."

Luke let that information sink in before he answered.

"St George? I miss them."

St George moved closer to Luke. "I'm sorry, Luke, that your parents were so cruelly taken from you. Close your eyes and concentrate."

Luke did so.

"Now, tell me. Can you see them?"

"Yes."

"Can you hear them?"

"Yes."

"And can you feel them?"

"Yes."

"Then they have left you not, Luke. Please remember that."

Luke opened his eyes, which had once again begun to tear up, and looked at St George. They smiled at each other and St George tenderly put his hand on Luke's shoulder.

"Well done, Luke Stevens. I return these to you."

St George held out both dragon's teeth.

Luke hesitated. "I don't want them. You have them."

"Alas, Luke. They are not mine to possess. You are the Chosen One and you are now tasked with keeping watch over them."

Luke reluctantly took them. He fastened one around his neck and put the other into his pocket.

"This is where I leave you, Luke Stevens. It has been an honour to meet you."

"You too, St George. Say hi to Florentia for me and thank her for the book."

"That I shall."

St George remounted his horse and began to trot away from the circle and the halo of light which seemed to be fading.

"Farewell, Luke Stevens. Until next time we meet."

"Bye, St George."

St George faded into the shadows and Luke watched him disappear. He began to walk towards Aunt Sarah and the others when he paused, turned around, and shouted.

"Wait! Next time?"

38

Luke made his way to Aunt Sarah just as she was stirring. He crouched down beside her and hugged her close, his wet face resting against hers. His tears combined with the cut on her head from where she'd been thrown against the rock. Luke was amazed to see that the cut was closing. Once it had completely vanished, all that remained was some of Aunt Sarah's dried blood. She opened her eyes and focused on Luke's face.

"Luke?"

"I'm here. It's okay. You're safe."

"What happened?"

"Maybe I should wait until everyone else has woken up."

Like Aunt Sarah, Carter, Patrick, Maria, Max, Felicity, Séamus, Pamela and the other Guardians were coming around, groggily shaking their heads and sitting up. The remaining members of Sebastian's evil army were still tied up together, unable to move. Luke stood up, which made him easy to spot. One by one, The Guardians noticed him standing there.

"Luke!" It was Patrick. "Oh, my boy. You did it! I knew you would, I just knew."

"Where's Sebastian?" asked Felicity.

Luke wasn't sure how to answer.

"He, err, he failed the test," was all he could think to say. He looked down sheepishly at his feet as he recalled the moment Sebastian had been dragged away, and shuddered. Silently, his friends came to him and took turns embracing him. Max was the last to do so.

"Well, Luke. We had quite an adventure. I want to thank you for, well, for everything you did for me. For all of us."

"Hear, hear," said Séamus.

The others all shared their agreement.

"Well, now," said Patrick. "It's been an eventful few days. On the assumption that things were going to go our way, I took the liberty of booking us into a Guardian hotel close to here. I dare say, Luke, you could do with some sleep?"

Luke was feeling anything but tired, but went along with it. "That would be great, Patrick."

"Splendid. I'll arrange some transportation for us and will contact the authorities to do something about Sebastian's men."

Patrick took out a telephone from his pocket and went to talk with one of the Guardians. Between them, they arranged cars to pick up some of their colleagues, whilst others made their own way home. In the distance, the flashing blue lights of police cars could be seen heading towards the monument.

Luke and his eight friends walked back to their respective vehicles, with Luke explaining exactly what had happened to him and Sebastian. Patrick insisted Luke described St George's appearance in as much detail as possible whilst he muttered, "amazing" or "remarkable" and the entire group stopped to embrace him again once he had told them of his choices and the visions of his parents.

"Luke, I'm sorry you were given this burden," said Patrick. "Your parents would be remarkably proud of you, as I know we are."

"Thanks, Patrick. I know they would be, too."

Luke reached up to touch the tooth around his neck and felt its comforting warmth.

"Patrick? Would you and Maria walk with me for a moment, please?" he asked.

"Of course, dear boy."

The three hung back a little from the others, Patrick and Maria exchanging curious glances with each other.

"Patrick, I'm so sorry that you're unwell," Luke said.

Patrick looked stunned, but knew better than to deny it. "How did you know?"

"Just a feeling. I think this tooth has enhanced more than my physical attributes."

"Remarkable, Luke." Patrick smiled fondly at him.

"I want you to have something." Luke reached into his pocket and pulled out the second tooth. He held it out for Patrick to take. "I know you don't have much time, however, with this tooth, you will have longer. Please, take it."

Patrick was dumbfounded and struggled for words.

"I can't take it, Luke. That tooth belongs to someone that has time on their side. My time has come and is about to go."

"Please, Patrick. I insist. You've been away from Maria for too long. It's only right you make up for the lost time."

"Luke, no."

"Maria, have a word, would you?"

"Luke's right, Patrick. We deserve it. Take the tooth, you silly old fool."

Patrick stared at the tooth with the leather cord running through it. He reached out his hand and clasped it, immediately feeling the warmth emanating from it. He closed his eyes and basked in its energy.

"Goodness," Patrick said. "I already feel 20 years younger." He then danced a brief Irish jig.

"So that makes you about 87, right?" teased Luke.

"Thank you for this, Luke. This silly old man has a lot of making up to do and he stands a good chance of doing it thanks to you," said Maria.

"Happy to help. I hope you enjoy your time together."

The three of them held each other and continued the journey to their cars and Patrick and Maria's motorbike and sidecar combination. They arrived and found that they had formed a circle and were all looking at each other with love and admiration. It was Pamela that broke the silence.

"Well, who knew that being a librarian could be so exciting?"

The group laughed and came together for one last moment, relishing each other's company. Patrick and Maria sped off with their laughter still audible long after they'd disappeared from sight. Max, Felicity, Séamus and Pamela were next to go, leaving Luke with Aunt Sarah and Carter.

"So," said Luke. "I never did finish my English homework."

"I think I might be able to write a note excusing you from that, given the circumstances," laughed Aunt Sarah. "Are you okay, Luke?"

"I am. It's been a weird few days, but I'm happy. I've met new people, made some friends and had a cosy chat with England's Patron Saint. Probably not normal for most 13-year-olds, but I guess my life was never destined to be normal."

Aunt Sarah could sense that there was something else on Luke's mind. "What's wrong, Luke? There's something you're not telling us."

Luke looked at Aunt Sarah and considered his answer.

"When I saw my parents, it felt so real. It was like they were there at that moment. I knew they couldn't be, but it was just so damn nice to think they might still be there. I know they're dead, okay. I understand that. But, for just a moment, I had them back again, and it felt right. And it felt fair."

Aunt Sarah looked at her nephew and had never felt more proud of him.

"You found out from an early age that life isn't always fair, Luke. But because of you, you've brought hope to millions of people. They might not know about what happened here tonight, but you know and we know."

"Luke, I too have lost my parents. I wasn't as young as you when it happened, but it still hurts, no matter your age. I think of them every day and I know they are here and here." Carter touched his head and his heart. "People die, but memories can live as long as you want them to. Hold on to that thought."

Luke nodded and smiled.

"Come on, Luke. Let's get some rest and tomorrow, we'll go home," said Aunt Sarah.

"Good idea. You'll come too, Carter?" asked Luke.

Carter and Aunt Sarah looked at each other, both not knowing what to say.

"Really?" said Luke. "Lost for words? Wow. You two are ridiculous. Yes, Luke. I'd love to move in with you and your aunt. Thank you for asking me to. There you go. Done."

Aunt Sarah and Carter began to laugh.

"Don't forget, I'm the Chosen One so what I say goes."

"Of course, almighty and powerful Chosen One," joked Aunt Sarah.

"Actually, can you call me the Chosen One from now on? I think it has a nice ring to it."

"Don't push it, Luke."

Aunt Sarah and Carter climbed into the car whilst Luke took one last look at the moon, its red glow fading by the minute. Reaching up to touch his tooth, he felt its warmth and closed his eyes. There they were. His parents smiling and waving at him. His dad's arm was around his mum's shoulders, and they were so full of joy. Luke gave a contented sigh and got into the car. He kept his eyes closed and his hand on the tooth all the way to the hotel. The smile never left his face, and he felt a serene peace embrace him. St George was right. His parents hadn't really left him, and he could see them whenever he wanted to. All Luke had to do was close his eyes.

EPILOGUE

They'd lost track of time. It could have been months since they had been taken, perhaps even years. The cells they were being kept in were dank and miserable and made from solid rock. Metal bars obstructed the only window in each of their rooms, which were high up and almost out of their reach. If they stood on their beds, they could just about see outside. Their view was of the ocean, which helped them stay sane. The crashing of the waves and the occasional bird call soothing their anxious minds.

Although their rooms were next to each other, they hadn't seen one another since they had been brought here. They'd tried talking, but their captor didn't like that and would beat them if they did. They were brought two meals a day, if you could call them meals. Just about enough to keep them healthy, which they did by exercising regularly during the day.

Every morning and every evening, they would communicate by using their cutlery to quietly tap on the bars of their windows. Morse code. It was simple, yet effective and their message was always the same; I love you. Stay strong. He will come.

Though they didn't know it, that message had been sent several thousand times over five years. Because that was how long the parents of Luke Stevens had been kept prisoner there.

The End

AFTERWORD

I do hope you've enjoyed reading about Luke and the Guardians. If you did, I'd appreciate it if you could take a few moments to leave a review on Amazon and / or Goodreads. Your reviews help more than you might realise. If you didn't enjoy it, please accept my apologies!

If you'd like to get in touch, please email ben@benpey ton.co.uk and head to www.benpeyton.co.uk for more about Luke, the Guardians and myself.

ACKNOWLEDGMENTS

My own Guardian, SJ, and our two Guardians-in-training, Lola and Jacob. My brother Jamie, Catherine, JJ and Niamh and my amazing parents for their emotional (and financial!) support. Since this was published back in April 2022, my heroic father, Séamus, has sadly died. My mum, Pamela, was his personal Guardian for over 50 years and continues to be an inspirational and incredible woman. I couldn't have asked for finer parents. Immortalising them in Luke's story was the least I could do.

Several people read about Luke and the Guardians when they were in the early stages and provided me with invaluable feedback. My gratitude to Alice Ashmore, Anna & Jack McNamara, Mary & Ariana Van Der Merwe, Helen Pope, Sarah Louise (have a look at her excellent book, *The Grubblers*), Vasilia Furnell-Petsas, Rob Cook, Emma Palmer and Becky & Lynne from House of Editors.

I'm grateful to my fantastic cover designer Tim from www.dissectdesigns.com for his creativity, enthusiasm and professionalism.

My thanks also to the spectacularly brilliant author, Rick Jones. Thanks for your advice, Rick, and also for your consistently superb books. Do have a look at Rick's thrillers (grown-ups only!). www.rickjonz.com

Finally, to bestselling author of some of my favourite books, *The Time Hunters*, Carl Ashmore. Thank you for your encouragement, patience and kindness. www.carlashmore.com

ABOUT THE AUTHOR

Ben Peyton is a former actor and now house-husband and writer. A keen movie watcher, Ben's film reviews have been published in Filmhounds Magazine, Time & Leisure Magazine and several online websites. You can read Ben's reviews at www.foryourfilmsonly.com and find him on Twitter @BenPeyton007.

Luke Stevens and the Blood of St George is Ben's debut novel.

LUKE STEVENS WILL RETURN...